LOVE I
INSPIRATIO

D0051361

Snowbound with the Amish Bachelor

PATRICIA JOHNS

Can she find a new place
in the world she left
behind?

LARGER PRINT

"You're pretty," he said.

No one had ever told her that before, and having Ben say it out loud made her heart tumble. That was what he thought when he looked at her.

"And that's me being too honest, I'm sure," he added.

"I don't mind," Grace said.

Was that some red in his cheeks she saw? He put a hand behind her back and nudged her farther away from the horse, his touch firm, protective.

"We should get this stable cleaned out," he said, clearing his throat.

"Yah." Her heart fluttered in her chest.

This time, it wasn't just her reacting. She'd seen the way he'd looked at her, and he was feeling it, too.

Maybe Grace should be a little more careful. She wasn't just a guest with an Amish background. She was here in a professional capacity to bring a baby girl back to the office.

Not to become emotionally entangled with this very available, very attractive man.

She had to remember that.

Patricia Johns is a *Publishers Weekly* bestselling author who writes from Alberta, Canada. She has her Hon. BA in English literature and currently writes for Harlequin's Love Inspired and Heartwarming lines. She also writes Amish romance for Kensington Books. You can find her at patriciajohnsromance.com.

Books by Patricia Johns

Love Inspired

Redemption's Amish Legacies

The Nanny's Amish Family
A Precious Christmas Gift
Wife on His Doorstep
Snowbound with the Amish Bachelor

Montana Twins

Her Cowboy's Twin Blessings
Her Twins' Cowboy Dad
A Rancher to Remember

Harlequin Heartwarming

The Second Chance Club

Their Mountain Reunion
Mountain Mistletoe Christmas
Rocky Mountain Baby

Visit the Author Profile page at Harlequin.com for more titles.

Snowbound with the Amish Bachelor

Patricia Johns

LOVE INSPIRED
INSPIRATIONAL ROMANCE

LOVE INSPIRED®
INSPIRATIONAL ROMANCE

Recycling programs
for this product may
not exist in your area.

ISBN-13: 978-1-335-56724-6

Snowbound with the Amish Bachelor

Copyright © 2021 by Patricia Johns

This edition published by arrangement with Harlequin Books S.A.

For questions and comments about the quality of this book, please contact us
at CustomerService@Harlequin.com.

Love Inspired
22 Adelaide St. West, 40th Floor
Toronto, Ontario M5H 4E3, Canada
www.Harlequin.com

Printed in U.S.A.

Then shall ye call upon me, and ye shall go and pray unto me, and I will hearken unto you.
—*Jeremiah* 29:12

To my husband. There's no one else I'd rather be snowed in with! I love you!

Chapter One

❧

Grace Schweitzer's cell phone, which was attached to a magnetic base on her car's dash, had no bars, and it had been that way for the last ten minutes. Funny how she'd become so dependent on her cell phone that losing service made her anxious. She'd never imagined that she'd be this way when she first got it.

Grace let out a slow breath, her gaze moving to the frost-touched fields on either side of the road. Barbed wire looped from fence post to fence post, and she spotted a large white hare standing tall on the edge of a field. He didn't blend in yet—the snow had held off this year.

The social services department where Grace worked had received a call about an abandoned baby. An Amish family had discovered an infant on their doorstep, and they'd called the officials—the right thing to do. Grace's supervisor would normally be with her on a case like this one, but the flu had made the rounds of the Vaughnville Social Services office, and Nadine was down sick. The town of Redemption and the Amish community that surrounded it were part of the greater Vaughnville area and fell under their jurisdiction. Grace was driving out to a distant Amish farm with a car seat secured into her back seat so that she could collect the baby.

No one at the office knew about Grace's Amish background—she didn't advertise it, as a rule. Yes, she'd been raised Amish, but left as a teenager so that she could pursue her education with the help of an *Englisher* aunt. And she'd never looked back. Her Amish upbringing had been in Creekside—an Amish community far enough away that she didn't know this Amish family personally. She was mildly relieved—explaining herself to acquaintances would not be comfortable. Besides, Grace's mother hadn't kept any secrets about where Grace was. She'd rounded up any praying woman she could find to add Grace's salvation to the prayer chain, a little fact that she'd shared with Grace on her last visit home.

A few flakes of snow were spinning from the sky by the time she slowed to a stop beside a mailbox with the name Hochstetler on the side. She looked down at the paper map on the passenger seat. This looked like the spot. She'd had to rely upon the physical map to get her the rest of the way to the farm, since her GPS didn't have a connection out here. Wi-Fi or satellite connection were details the Amish wouldn't even notice.

Grace turned up the drive and had to step on the brakes as a turkey wandered across the gravel and strutted in the direction of the stable. A side door opened as she pulled up and parked, and a tall, broad-shouldered man stood in the doorway, a hat on his head, his sleeves rolled up his forearms. He didn't react to the cold—just stood there, watching her.

"Hello!" Grace called as she got out of the vehicle. "I'm Grace Schweitzer from Vaughnville Social Services. Are you Ben Hochstetler?"

"*Yah*, that's me," the man replied. "Thank you for coming."

The snow was falling faster now, and Grace looked at the sky uncertainly. The forecast had only called for light snow today and the storm was supposed to miss them, but the dense cloud cover and rising wind didn't bode well for her drive back. The quicker she could get started, the better.

She unbuckled the car seat from the back seat and carried it toward the side door, where the tall man waited. He was good-looking—tall, broad, with dark eyes that moved over her in unrepentant curiosity. His face was shaven, so he was single, too. He held the door open and stood back to let her come inside. They passed through a mudroom with rubber boots lined up on shelves and coats on hooks, alongside a deep sink for washing up. Then they emerged into a traditional Amish kitchen.

Grace felt a wave of nostalgia as she looked around—it could have been her mother's kitchen if it had been in Creekside. There were the same tall cupboards, the heavy wooden table and a wooden bread box on the counter that read God Bless This Home in Pennsylvania Dutch. A single clock was on the wall, ticking loudly, and a young woman stood by the stove, a blanket-wrapped baby in her arms.

"Come in," Ben said. "This is my sister, Iris."

"Hello," Grace said with a smile, careful to keep to English. She was here for professional purposes, not to have her faith, or lack thereof, judged by strangers.

"She arrived in this basket," Ben said, and he picked up an Amish woven basket from a corner. There were a bottle, a soother and a couple more blankets inside.

"How did you find her?" Grace asked. "How long was she outside?"

"We were having breakfast—it was before dawn," Ben replied. "There was a knock on the door, and we heard a baby's cry, and then a car engine. When we opened the door, the baby was there and a car was just disappearing up the drive. So she wasn't out here alone more than a moment."

"That's a good thing." Grace breathed. "Can I see the baby?"

Iris came forward and passed the infant into Grace's arms. The baby was only about three or four months old, and she squirmed as Grace took her, scrunching up her face and letting out a plaintive cry. She wasn't very big, and her eyes were a dark blue. Her hair—the tiny wisps on top of her velvet head—were honey-blond.

"I think it's warmer over here," Grace said. She headed over to the large black stove, and the baby settled again. She glanced back to see Ben and Iris standing side by side, and Grace could see the family resemblance between them. They both had dark hair and dark eyes, the same determined set to their mouths, the same shape of nose. The baby's diaper gurgled and Grace smiled wanly. "She's going to need a change. I brought a package of diapers—it's in my trunk."

"I'll get it for you," Ben said. "Keys?"

Grace pulled the keys from her coat pocket and tossed them across the kitchen. Ben caught them neatly in his palm. For just a split second he shot her a grin, and her heart skipped a beat. She really shouldn't be noticing his good looks, but it was hard not to. There was something about the spontaneous laughter in his eyes as the smile split his face. Then he turned and headed out the door.

"What will happen to her?" Iris asked softly, and her voice pulled Grace back to the work at hand.

"Well…" Grace looked down at the baby's face. "I'll bring her to the social services office, and there will be some doctors' visits to make sure she's healthy and doing okay. Then she'll go to a foster home, where another family will take care of her."

"And the mother?"

Grace shrugged. "The police will look for her. It's a delicate situation."

Iris nodded. "I can't imagine just dropping my baby off with strangers—"

Grace looked down at the little Disney-patterned sleeper. "By the looks of the clothes, I'd say this is an *Englisher* baby."

"Yah," Iris agreed. "We don't use their patterns."

"I know it will seem strange to you, but the *Englishers* think that Amish families are..." Grace searched for a way to describe it. "They think Amish families are kinder and more Christian, somehow. And if this *Englisher* mother brought her baby all the way to an Amish farm, I think in her own way she was trying to do the best she could for her child."

Iris was silent for a beat, and then the door opened and Ben came back inside. He pulled off his hat and shook snow off the brim.

"It's snowing hard now," he said in Pennsylvania Dutch. Then he glanced at Grace and switched to English. "Sorry, I just said that it's really snowing."

Grace moved toward the window, and she could see snow coming down in swirling gusts. It had started up quickly, and she felt a shiver work its way up her spine. The roads were going to be miserable already. A man came past the window, and Grace startled.

"Oh, that's my father," Ben said. "He was out at the barn."

His beard was long and gray, but he wasn't very tall. The side door opened again and the man came inside. He stamped his boots, and the water turned on at the sink, but Grace couldn't see inside the mudroom from where she stood.

"Where should we change her?" Grace asked.

"I can do it," Iris said with a smile. "I'm getting married in three weeks, so I could use some practice."

Grace smiled at that. Back when she was a teen, she used to think of caring for her younger siblings and cousins as practice for when she'd be caring for her own children, too. Maybe if she'd stayed Amish, Grace would be married by now, but out in the big, wide world of *Englishers*, she hadn't found anyone yet. And that was one part about having left the Amish life that she missed. She knew how love and marriage worked in Amish communities, and she was still trying to figure it out with the *Englishers*.

Iris took the baby from Grace's arms and smiled down into the little face, and Ben passed his sister the plastic package of diapers.

"We're going to get you cleaned up, little one," Iris said in Dutch, just as their father came into the kitchen.

"That'll be a blizzard, all right," the old

man said in Dutch, and both Ben and Iris looked toward the window. Then he added in English, "Hello, my name is Hannes. You must be from the social services office. My son was the one who called."

"Pleasure to meet you," Grace said, and she reached out to shake his hand. Iris left the room with the baby.

"Did you see the letter yet?" Hannes asked.

"What letter?" she asked.

"The one that came with the baby." Hannes went to the counter and picked up an envelope. He pulled out a piece of paper, then passed her the handwritten note.

Please take care of my baby girl. Her name is Taylor, and I love her more than anything, but I won't be able to take care of her the way I should. I know it already. The longer I wait to give her up, the harder it will be, so I'm doing it now. I pray that you're the right family. Tell her that her mama loves her.

There was no signature, and the handwriting looked almost childish. The mother might not be very old, Grace realized with a sinking heart. There was so much pain in this line of work, but at least she could do something to help.

"It's sad, isn't it?" Hannes said quietly.

"It is." Grace swallowed a tightness in her throat, folded the page again and tucked it back into the envelope. "The police will want to see this. I'll bring it back to the office with me."

"I wish we could have done what the young mother wanted," Hannes said. "But Iris there is getting married in three weeks, and Ben is leaving right after his sister's wedding. That leaves me—and while I do love *bobbilies*, I'll be a man alone. I'm not the right one to bring up a little girl by myself."

"That's understandable," Grace said. "And no one is expecting you to do that."

"The mother seems to be," he replied quietly.

"You did the right thing calling us," Grace replied.

"I hope so." He sighed. "If she comes back looking for her little one, I'm going to feel terrible if I have to tell her that we sent her away." Hannes turned toward his son and switched to Dutch. "Have you offered her anything to eat yet?"

"No," Ben replied, also in Dutch. "She just arrived."

"That's why you're still single," Hannes said, shaking a teasing finger in his son's direction.

"You'd have me sweet-talking an *Englisher*?" Ben asked, spreading his hands, but there was humor in his eyes. "I thought you wanted me to go find a good Amish girl? Huh?"

Hannes rolled his eyes and chuckled, then switched back to English. "I'm no expert on driving cars, young lady, but I wouldn't take a team of horses out onto the roads in that storm."

Grace went to the window again and looked out. A gust of snow whirled past the glass, whiting out her view completely. The storm had come from nowhere, and it was picking up speed. How long could this last? Another hour? She looked back toward the older man helplessly.

"I'm not sure it's safe to drive in that, either," she admitted. "The weather channel didn't call for snow." She pulled her cell phone out of her pocket and looked down at the reception. There was none. She lifted the phone higher and walked around the room a little. Still nothing.

"Oh, that won't work here," Hannes said.

"Why?" she asked.

"I don't know the technical term, but we call it a blessed spot," Hannes said. "It's one place in this county where none of those gadgets seem to work, and you're forced to rely upon your own senses and directions from the neighbors."

"Right." Grace smiled wanly. *Dead spot* was the term he was looking for, but from the Amish perspective, there was nothing terrible about no cell phone service or GPSs that wouldn't function.

"How did you call us?" Grace asked. Was there an *Englisher* neighbor close by, perhaps? Ben had managed to call the social services office when he'd needed to, and while she couldn't expect anyone to drive out here in this storm, she could at least let them know she was all right.

"Oh, there's an Amish phone booth about five miles that way." Hannes pointed toward the window. "It's just outside an *Englisher* farm. He's a friend of ours—Steve Mills. Ben took the buggy to make the call."

And in a blowing storm, going that five miles to the phone booth would be foolish for her to attempt. Her feeble surge of hope sank back down. What would she do now? She looked up, and Ben's direct gaze locked onto hers. Her breath caught.

"You can stay with us until the storm passes," Ben said.

"Of course," Hannes agreed. "I doubt it will last too long."

There wasn't much else Grace could do. She couldn't bring a baby out into dangerous road conditions. Even alone, she wouldn't want to risk it. And as unprofessional as it was to admit, the invitation coming from Ben was rather tempting.

"Thank you," she said at last. "I appreciate that."

Ben met Grace's gaze, and she smiled. The smile transformed her face in an instant—she was incredibly pretty, and there was something about the easy way she stood inside their home, too, almost like she belonged in an Amish environment. Obviously, she didn't—dressed in a plum-colored pantsuit that fit her slim figure perfectly. Amish women didn't wear pants, and they seemed almost scandalous. So her belonging here was very likely his imagination.

"Have a seat," Ben said, gesturing to a kitchen chair. "Are you hungry? We've got pie, some apple crisp—" He glanced toward the ice box. "I could make you a sandwich?"

"Oh, I'm fine for now," she said. "Thanks, though."

Ben went to the stove to get a pot of hot

coffee, and his father ambled in his direction. He glanced back at Grace—her wavy brown hair pulled back away from her face, exposing her creamy neck.

"Get her something to eat," Hannes said in Dutch.

"She said she'd doesn't want anything," he replied, pulling his attention away from her.

"She's being polite," Hannes said. "I like to think I raised you better than that!"

"I'll bring her pie," Ben said. "Happy?"

"Do you want coffee?" his father asked in English, turning toward Grace and raising his voice.

"Please," Grace replied.

"See?" his father said, casting Ben a meaningful look, as if that explained things.

"I asked her—" Ben sighed. "Yah. Fine. I'll bring her pie and coffee. But honestly, *Daet*, I don't know why you're so set on me charming an *Englisher*."

"You need some practice with charm, period," his father replied, casting him a teasing smile. "I need five or six more grandchildren, and I'm not sending you to your uncle to act like a gruff farmer. I want you coming home with a wife. This house needs it."

Ben chuckled. It was an old conversation, and while they bantered about it, his father had a point. Ben hadn't warmed up to any of the girls here. There were plenty of young women his age, but they were relatives, and the three girls who weren't related to him just didn't interest him. A more reasonable man would pick the best of the three and try to find something deeper there...but maybe Ben wasn't reasonable enough, because he'd been praying for the whole package—a woman he could love with all his heart, who was Amish to the core.

Surely, *Gott* could provide the modern equivalent of a Biblical Rebecca to his Isaac—an Amish woman who would fill his heart. This was the reason he was going to Shipshewana, Indiana, right after his sister's wedding to visit his uncle. He wanted to find a wife of his own. At least, that was his prayer.

"Do you want pie and coffee, too, *Daet*?" Ben asked.

"Don't mind if I do."

Ben cut three generous slices of pie and dished them onto plates. He poured three mugs of coffee and brought them to the table. When he slid a plate in front of Grace, he said, "My father insists that you're hungry."

"This does look good." She smiled ruefully and accepted a fork. "Thanks."

Hannes's smile was self-satisfied. "I was married for thirty-five years, son," he said in Dutch. "You should trust me."

Ben's gaze flickered toward Grace. She didn't look up. They were being rude, speaking in a language she didn't understand. Was it unreasonable that he was the smallest bit annoyed that he hadn't realized she was only being polite first? A man in his sixties shouldn't be better at these things.

"My father is just congratulating himself on knowing you were hungry after all," Ben said.

Grace looked up. "He's good."

"He thinks so," Ben said, and he shot his father a grin.

Iris came back into the kitchen, the baby awake in her arms. "Do I smell coffee?" she asked.

"Yah," Ben said, dishing his sister up a slice of pie and pushing it toward Iris's seat at the table. He'd miss having his sister in the family home when she got married. When he came back, if all went according to plan, everything would be different, though. He'd hopefully have his own bride.

"You hold the baby," Iris said, passing the infant over, and Ben awkwardly adjusted her in his arms. Taylor—that's what the letter said the little girl's name was—settled into his arms, and he looked down at those wide blue eyes and the downy blond hair.

"Hello," he murmured in English. He tucked her up onto his shoulder and adjusted the blanket around her. She snuggled into his chest, and he felt a wave of protectiveness for the little thing. How could her mother have left her like that? As if the baby had been thinking of her mother, too, she screwed up her face and started to cry.

"Hey, there," Ben said, jiggling her. "Hey... Hey..."

He didn't know what to do. He wasn't her mother, and he doubted that any of them would be enough to soothe this baby properly.

"Hold her like this—" His father mimed holding the baby on her back. "Go on."

Ben glanced toward Grace, who was watching him with a curious look on her face, and he did as his father said. Hannes swung back and forth, mimicking the movement he wanted Ben to make. Ben did as his father indicated, and the baby soothed again, sucking in a long, shuddering breath. All day long, Hannes had been the one giving tips on how to soothe the baby, and almost every time he'd been right.

"Yah, yah, that's it," Hannes said.

Grace watched the older man with a look of new respect in her eyes.

"I've raised six of my own," Hannes said by explanation. "A man learns a thing or two about soothing babies."

"My *daet* is the favorite *dawdie*—" Ben began, and then caught himself and adjusted his phrasing to remove the Dutch words. "Sorry, my father is the favorite grandfather. He has—how many grandchildren now?"

"Eighteen grandchildren," Hannes said. "And I've put every single one of them to sleep."

"He has the touch," Iris said, sipping her coffee. "When we have family gatherings, there's always a fussy baby—sometimes two or three. And *Dawdie* here picks up that baby and rocks and cuddles him until he's quiet as a lamb."

Grace smiled at that. "Every family needs an expert."

The baby's eyes started to close, and Ben slowed his rocking. He looked around—the only place to put the baby was in the basket that she'd arrived in, and that felt wrong. This little girl had already been through too much, and putting her back into the basket that had separated her from her mother felt unreasonably cruel.

Outside the window, the snow fell even more heavily, and a low wind moaned. Ben stood up and went to the window to get a better view, and he saw Grace's car, two small drifts of snow already forming on one side of it against the wheels. This baby wasn't leaving the house anytime soon, and if he was right, both she and the social service agent would be here for the night, at least. Was it selfish of him to like the idea? Call it boredom, or just being ready for a change in his life, but the company in the house—especially such pretty company—would be welcome.

"We need the cradle from the attic," Ben said.

"*Yah*, that would be a good idea." His father put his last bite of pie into his mouth.

"And I need to get dinner started," Iris said, standing up with her plate.

Grace's gaze moved toward the basket.

"*Daet*, why don't you hold the baby, and I'll go find the cradle," Ben said. "Grace, if you wanted to come help me, it'll go faster."

"Sure." Grace rose to her feet. "I'd be happy to."

It had been an impulsive request—he could have just as easily asked Grace to hold the baby, but he liked the idea of talking to her a little bit more. Ben eased the baby into his father's arms. Hannes made some shushing noises, and little Taylor settled again. Ben paused for a moment, watching her. Then he nodded toward the staircase.

"This way," he said.

Grace joined him, and she smiled up at him. What was it about that smile that gave his heart a tumble? He'd better be careful not to be foolhardy here. She was an *Englisher*, and pretty as she was, she'd only be a guest here. Nothing more. But maybe his *daet* was right, and he could use some practice being likable.

The attic trapdoor was located in the ceiling of the second-floor hallway. The upstairs was dim, though, even in the middle of the day, and he opened his bedroom door and retrieved his kerosene lamp. He lit the lamp with a match. The warm glow illuminated Grace's features. She was more than pretty. She was beautiful.

Grace pulled her cell phone out of her slacks pocket and looked down at the screen.

"Looking for service still?" he asked.

She blushed slightly. "Thought I'd check."

"You won't find it," he said. "Sorry..." He paused. "I know we're strangers, and I know this wasn't your plan, but you are safe here."

She smiled wanly. "Of course. I'm not afraid."

The fact that she'd mentioned fear at all made him wonder if perhaps she was. Was she frightened stuck out here so far from her home and her job?

"It'll be okay." He rubbed a hand over the stubble on his chin. "It doesn't look like the storm is going to let up anytime soon, either. So it might be best to just get comfortable."

"We'll see." She looked toward the window again. "Sometimes storms stop as quickly as they come up."

And sometimes they lasted for days. But she wanted to get out of their house and back to her own, no doubt.

"I imagine your family is going to be worried," he said, and he glanced down at her left hand. *Englishers* wore wedding rings if they were married, but her hand was bare.

"My boss will be," she said.

He licked his lips. "No one else?"

No husband? No fiancé? No man who'd be racked with worry when she didn't contact him?

"I live alone," she said with a faint shrug. "But if the office doesn't hear from me, they'll contact the police, and probably my aunt—" She stopped.

"Well, they know where to find you, *yah*?"

He pushed a thumb under his suspender. "You'll be safe enough until the snow stops and we dig out."

Grace smiled at that. "I feel terrible imposing on your family like this."

She felt bad for being here? Well, she and baby Taylor downstairs were the most interesting event that had happened on this farm in the last decade.

"We called you," he said. "Blame the weather, if you have to blame something."

Ben reached up, and grabbed the short rope that attached to the attic door, and pulled it down. A set of steep, narrow stairs unfolded and hit the wooden floor with a soft *thunk*.

"I don't know if you believe in *Gott* or not," he said, climbing up the steps, the lantern held aloft. "But we have a way of thinking here in Plain country. We don't need much to be happy—our daily bread, a roof over our heads and a family to love us. And when storms come—" He emerged into the attic, his feet still on the stairs and his voice echoing around him.

There were boxes, some old canning jars, a broken bedstead, and to his left, the cradle. He reached for it and pulled it closer, the heavy wood scraping against the thin floor.

He descended a few steps and saw Grace on the bottom step behind him, looking up.

"Hold this," he said, handing down the lantern. She took it and held it high, and Ben went back up and grabbed the cradle, hoisting it over one shoulder before he backed down the narrow stairs. She descended behind him, and he lowered the solid wooden cradle to the floor.

"There." He pushed the folding stairs, and they disappeared up with a spring to pull them.

"There," she echoed.

"And when storms come," he said, to complete his thought, "as long as we have our faith and our family, we simply ride it out."

Grace nodded. "No choice, I suppose."

"Well, there's always a choice," he said. "But railing against the weather is seldom helpful."

Grace chuckled.

"Grace, you'll likely be here until tomorrow," Ben said, sobering. "I'm just being honest here. I know you'd rather be home tonight, but we have an extra bed in Iris's room from when she used to share it with our older sister, and Iris has some clothes you can borrow. Don't spend this evening worrying about whether or not you'll be a burden. Because you aren't. Okay?"

"Thank you," she said. "I do appreciate it."

"We can turn that lamp off—"

Without being told how, she turned the knob, and the flame went out. He eyed her for a moment, and she met his gaze without a blink. Ben picked up the cradle again in one hand—and if he had to be honest, he was showing off a little bit. The cradle was heavy, but he wouldn't let her know it. They made their way down the stairs. There was a storm outside, but the house was warm, and this evening, they had not only a baby girl in need of care but also a houseguest in need of hospitality.

Chapter Two

"*Yah*, that's the one," Hannes said in Dutch as they came down the stairs.

Grace reached the bottom of the stairs just behind Ben, who hoisted the cradle, then swung it up so he could catch the other side of it and put it down gently next to the table. He was strong—that was obvious—and she tried to appear like she hadn't noticed the bulge of his muscles. The cradle was solid and low, with rockers so that the baby could be rocked to sleep with one foot while the caregiver did some other chore at the same time.

Babies were treasured in Amish homes, and thoroughly loved, but work had to go on.

"Use the quilt on the back of the sofa to put in the bottom," Iris said.

"What about the one—" Ben started.

"No, no, use the one I said," Iris interrupted.

"Just trust me. And get one of her blankets that was left with her to go on top of her for now."

The family was talking in Dutch, and Grace moved over to the window, looking out at the drifting snow. She understood a family's tendency to chat in their mother tongue when they weren't used to *Englisher* visitors. Her family did this, too. They thought their idle conversation was private, and it seemed rude to let them in on the fact that she could understand them. Let them chat. Grace would be gone soon enough, anyway. Besides, she didn't want to explain herself. The Amish saw the English in a particular way. They were kind to them, even indulgent. But an Amish woman who'd left the faith and abandoned the narrow path? She wouldn't get the same indulgence. She knew that from her incredibly strained relationship with her own parents, and Grace didn't want to go over her reasons for making the choices she had with strangers—even kind ones.

Grace's gaze stopped at her car. The snow was domed on top, and the whole side of it was nearly covered in a snowbank. Some windows were still clear because the snow kept slipping off the glass. Then another rush of snow whipped past the window, blocking her view.

Lord, please stop the storm, she prayed silently. *Let me get back home.*

As if in reply, another gust of howling wind rattled the window.

Was that a no?

Grace's *mamm* would see this as *Gott* working—bringing her back to a house of faith and locking her in by use of a storm. Her *mamm* would interpret this as an answer to years of prayer sent up by both of her parents after Grace had left the faith. Her parents believed in prayer, and so did Grace, but their prayers often seemed at odds. Her parents prayed for her to come back and become the person she used to be. She prayed for them to understand why she couldn't. But her *mamm* had always prayed with fierce devotion. She spent an hour every morning on her knees before she even started her daily chores. She could be found praying alone in the sitting room late at night in her nightgown.

And that earnest, stubborn, narrowly focused prayer irritated Grace more than anything else. Maybe *Gott* didn't want Grace back in the fold with the rest of the Amish! But that hadn't occurred to either of her parents, and it never would.

Grace turned back to the kitchen. Iris had pulled potatoes and carrots out of a cupboard, and she put a cutting board down next to them.

"Can I help you with anything, Iris?" Grace asked.

"*Yah*, that would be nice," Iris said. "I can get you to peel carrots and then grate them for the cabbage salad."

Grace took off her suit jacket and hung it over a chair. She washed her hands and then picked up the peeler and the first of the carrots. As her hands worked, she watched as Ben put a folded quilt into the bottom of the cradle. He was careful, adjusting the corners and smoothing it down. Hannes laid the baby inside, and both men froze for a moment while the infant settled. They straightened at the same time. She couldn't help but smile at that.

"Do you want to borrow an apron?" Iris asked, pulling Grace's attention back.

Iris lifted a white Amish apron from a drawer, and Grace's heart skipped a beat. An apron... It had been a good many years since she'd worn one. An Amish apron was more than a tool in the kitchen—it was a statement of faith, part of a well-put-together woman. When Grace visited her parents, she wouldn't wear one. It was too fraught with meaning, and it had felt like giving her parents false hope.

"No, I'm fine," she said, her voice feeling tight.

"Are you sure?" Iris touched the silk of Grace's blouse. "This looks like it wouldn't wash easily."

"I'll be careful," Grace said with a faint smile.

Iris shrugged, letting it go. "Are you married?"

"No, I'm not," Grace said.

"Boyfriend?"

"No." Grace smiled. "Just me. I'd love to hear about your wedding, though. How did you meet him?"

"He's our neighbor," Iris replied. "They're the next farm over, so I've known him all my life. They're actually out of town right now, visiting a favorite aunt in Lititz. It's her ninetieth birthday, and she won't be able to travel for the wedding. Caleb and I will go see her after we're married, because I'd love to meet her."

"I hope they aren't caught in the storm," Grace said.

"They aren't due back for a few days, so they'll know to hold off," she replied.

"You must be excited," Grace said.

"*Yah.* I am." Iris shot her a smile. "So, how do *Englishers* find their husbands?"

Grace wished she knew. "Uh—" She felt some heat come to her cheeks. "I'm not much of an expert on that."

"But I mean, there must be ordinary paths," Iris pressed. "We Amish tend to meet at youth events, and then the boy will drive the girl home. Or you live next to him…or your families are particular friends. And when they get to know each other well enough, he'll ask her to marry him."

So simple. So straightforward. In fact, Grace's sister had been engaged at the time of her death, and she'd left a grieving fiancé behind. Going on to get married herself felt almost like a betrayal to her older sister. Tabitha would never get married now.

"Well, I have some friends who met their boyfriends at work," Grace said. "One friend met her boyfriend on vacation—they were part of the same tourist group. And some meet at church."

"Church is a good place," Iris said with an affirming nod. "Faith is important."

Grace looked up, and she found Ben's gaze resting on her. He smiled faintly when he was caught, but he didn't drop his gaze.

"They meet somewhere, and then they…

court?" Ben said. "What do you do instead of buggy rides to sort things out? I spent some time in Pittsburgh, but I wasn't dating English girls."

Those buggy rides were important. It was a chance for a couple to be alone and to talk. It was a chance to see if there was a spark.

"They sit in cars," Grace replied.

"Oh." Ben nodded. "Seems like it would be uncomfortable. With reins, you know what to do with your hands."

"They fiddle with the radio buttons," Grace said, and she laughed softly. "It's not so different, really." She felt the room's attention on her, and she licked her lips. "It's like anywhere. Who is to say what it is that draws a couple together? They fall in love, and they just know."

The baby let out a soft sound, not quite a cry, and Ben gently rocked the cradle. The movement seemed to work, because the baby's whimpers stopped.

"*Yah*, you just know…" Iris said with a gentle smile.

Grace watched the young woman for a moment, and then sighed. It wasn't really as easy as she was making it sound. It seemed to work for others. *Englisher* girls seemed to understand the code. For example, if a young man asked a girl out for coffee, that meant something. And if he had a beard, that meant nothing at all—just that he liked the style. She never could adjust to spending time with a bearded man. It felt wrong still. Bearded men were married men for the Amish.

Grace picked up the next carrot and continued to peel.

"We're trying to get Ben here married off," Iris said after a moment of silence. "He might not seem difficult when you look at him, but he's not an easy one to match."

"How come?" Grace asked, glad to change the topic away from herself. And Iris was right. To look at Ben, he was a handsome man—tall, strong, muscled.

"Because I'm related to too many girls in the area," Ben said with a laugh. "It isn't my fault."

"Oh, it's more than that." Iris chuckled. "He doesn't seem to notice when girls flirt with him. So he's going to a new community right after my wedding. And he'll have to learn how to be nice."

"I'm nice!" Ben countered.

"And how to flirt with girls," Iris said, rolling her eyes. "He's too serious. He's too honest. He just says whatever is in his head, and that will not help him find a wife."

A little honesty actually sounded nice, Grace had to admit. She was tired of trying to guess what was happening in a man's head, especially with *Englishers*. She had trouble reading them.

"I'm sure he'll manage it," Grace said. It was hard to imagine Ben struggling with women at all.

"You see?" Ben said to his sister in Dutch. "She thinks I'll be fine."

"She's being polite," Iris shot back with a laugh. "But you'll be new, and I imagine the girls there will be glad enough to have someone fresh to consider, if you can just remember to be nice."

Grace suppressed a smirk.

"My sister doesn't think I'm nice enough," Ben said, switching back to English. "But you don't have to worry about me. I'm not half so bad as they make me sound."

Hannes rose to his feet. "It's not letting up."

"No, it's not." Ben's gaze followed his father's toward the window.

"Let's go check the barn, then," Hannes said. "The cattle will need some extra hay out in the field, as well."

"*Yah*, they will." Ben rose to his feet. The men turned toward the door, and

Hannes picked up an empty baby bottle from the table and waggled it between his fingers.

"She'll need another one of these when she wakes up," the older man said.

"I know, *Daet*," Iris said in Dutch. "Don't worry. It's under control."

When the men plunged their feet into their rubber boots and the door closed solidly behind them, the baby started to fuss again. Grace put down her peeler and went over to the cradle. She lifted the baby and snuggled her close. Taylor pulled her knees up and wriggled, her little mouth opening in the shape of an O.

"We always have some formula on hand," Iris said, pulling a can down from a cupboard. "We didn't have to run to a neighbor to borrow any when this baby arrived on the doorstep. Two of my sisters have babies right now, and a third one is pregnant out to here." She measured with her hand, an obvious exaggeration, and the younger woman laughed softly.

While Iris went about preparing the bottle, Grace ran her hand over the baby's downy head, her heart reaching out around the little thing. She needed more than milk, more than warmth and comfort. She needed love.

Grace looked out the side window, and she

saw the men trudging through the blowing snow past the house. Their heads were down, the driving snow hitting the tops of their hats. They grimaced against the onslaught. And then, Ben looked toward the house, and his gaze met hers with such directness that it took her breath away. It couldn't have lasted more than a second, but it was like his gaze had drilled right through her.

"Here you are."

Grace startled and looked over to find Iris handing her a warmed baby bottle.

"Thanks," she said, and she looked toward the window once more. Ben and Hannes were past the house now, and she could only see their backs.

Grace smiled down into the hungry face of the baby, and she popped the nipple into her searching mouth. Taylor started to suck. A little dribble of milk ran down her chin, and Grace used the corner of the blanket to wipe it away. Those blue eyes, dark as navy, locked onto her face as the baby drank.

Grace couldn't forget that she was here to bring a baby back to a foster family. And handsome or not, Ben Hochstetler wasn't her business. He had plans for his future, and so did she. The Amish life might sink down to her bones, but it wasn't a part of her future.

* * *

Ben reined the quarter horses in and jumped down from the wagon. He'd just delivered three large bales of hay to the cattle in the field. There was a copse of trees that sheltered the small herd from the storm, but the extra silage would help the cattle keep their body heat up during the worst of it.

The wind whisked a veil of snow past his eyes, and Ben squeezed them shut, his face numb from the continuous blast of cold. But the cattle would be fine, and they were his primary concern right now. Or they were supposed to be. His mind kept moving back to the women at the house...one woman in particular.

It was silly that just when he was getting ready to leave Redemption behind and start a new life away from here, he'd finally see a woman who intrigued him. An *Englisher* woman...and maybe he deserved that irony. Because he had fallen in love once, but that was when he was young and stupid, and he'd brought his girlfriend with him to the city on their *Rumspringa*. More than a proper *Rumspringa*—they'd left home and gone to Pittsburgh together, and Charity Lapp hadn't returned with him. She'd decided to stay—the *Englisher* world suited her, after all.

So he really didn't know how *Englishers* dated or found romantic partners. The time he'd spent in Pittsburgh, he'd had Charity, and she'd been a comfort because it meant he didn't have to leave his Amish life completely behind him. It hadn't taken him more than a few months to realize his monumental mistake and go home. He'd never suspected that Charity would decide to stay.

So here he was, ready to go start his life and choose a good Amish girl, put his mistakes firmly behind him…and an *Englisher* woman—one who was distractingly pretty and felt like a puzzle—ended up on his doorstep.

Maybe he deserved it.

"Good work, boys," Ben murmured to the horses, and he set about unhitching them so that he could bring them into the warm shelter of the stable.

His father was in the barn still, tending to the goats, a cow that had injured its leg in a gopher hole, some calves and their milk cow. Hannes couldn't run this farm alone, but Ben had the reassurance that when his sister got married, Caleb and Iris would be here with *Daet* to work the farm together. That was how Amish marriages traditionally worked—the first year was spent with the bride's family while the new couple sorted out where they'd live afterward.

Otherwise, Ben couldn't leave his father alone with this amount of work.

Ben brought the horses into the stable and got them set up with extra oats. When he came back outside, he heard a bang and saw the door to the chicken coop flap open in the wind. The chicken coop was a stout little building that allowed the farmer to go inside to collect eggs.

"Great," he muttered, and he held his hat down with one hand as he headed in that direction. There was a light inside, though—the bobbing illumination of a kerosene lamp—and when he got to the coop, he stopped short in surprise.

He was expecting to see his sister out there, but it wasn't. Grace was swathed in one of Ben's extra coats, and she was squatting down, pushing hay into some cracks in the coop wall.

"Grace?"

Grace looked up. Her shoulder-length, wavy hair was tousled, and she shot him a tired smile.

"We saw the coop door swinging free, and your sister is cooking, so I offered to come take care of it," Grace said.

"Thank you," he said. He hadn't expected her to take the initiative like that, but he was glad she had.

He did a quick count of the chickens, and all nine seemed to be there—including one rebellious little hen sitting on a rafter. The rooster strutted about, pecking at some grain on the floor, entirely unperturbed by the storm. Ben pulled the door shut behind him and put the hook in place to keep it secure. The wind rattled it as it whistled past the coop, and he squatted down next to her, helping her stuff the cracks with straw. Her dress pants had a smear of dust down one side already.

"There," she breathed as they finished the last of a long crack. The coop already felt warmer, and outside, the wind howled in defiance.

Ben rose to his feet, and when she struggled to get her balance to stand, he held out a hand to her. Grace put her bare fingers in his gloved hand, and he tugged her to her feet. Her fingers were red with cold, and he pulled off his gloves and handed them to her.

"No, you've got work—" she started.

"We're going in," he said. "I've done what I needed to do for now. Put them on."

She smiled faintly and pulled the gloves

onto her hands. His coat was big on her, enveloping her frame, and standing there in her *Englisher* office clothes, a pair of Iris's rubber boots on her feet and a piece of straw stuck in her hair, she looked uncomfortably endearing. He'd expected an *Englisher* woman to sit inside the house and wait, not throw herself into helping out like this.

"You aren't what I expected," he said.

"What did you expect?" she asked, raising her eyebrows.

"You're tougher than I thought," he admitted.

She laughed softly. "This is that raw honesty your sister was talking about."

"Yah." His family enjoyed teasing him just a little too much. Would it kill them to let him save face in front of his pretty guest?

"It's okay," she said, seeming to misread his silence. "I don't mind being called tough."

"What made you think to stuff the cracks?" Ben asked. He'd been planning to do the same thing himself.

"I grew up on a farm."

So that explained it. She would be tougher than *Englisher* city girls. And maybe that was why he felt a draw toward her. That would make it understandable, at least, because he knew what was good for him, and that wasn't some passing *Englisher* woman.

"You live in the city now, though," he said.

"Yes, I live in Vaughnville," she replied. "In an apartment, no less, where all I can grow are some potted plants on my balcony."

He smiled ruefully. "Flowers?"

In his time in Pittsburgh, he remembered those balcony gardens that people grew—their railings lined with flower planters. Even in the city, people longed for greenery and blossoms...

"Some cherry tomatoes, some peas, a single strawberry plant," she replied, and he thought he saw some sadness in her gaze. Then she shrugged. "It's a much different life."

"Do you prefer it?" he asked. "To life on the farm, I mean."

Did she like those tiny balconies that offered a postage-stamp size of nature? Did she like concrete and exhaust, the constant fast pace and the endless fast food?

"I can make a difference there." Her gaze turned serious. "And that's what matters most to me. I want to—" she cast her glance around the coop "—I want to make things easier for people, help heal some pain. I want to provide solutions."

"*Yah*, you do that," he said. That was why she was here, after all, wasn't it? She was *their* solution to a problem. "So what unsolvable problems drove you to this line of work?"

She eyed him uncertainly. "Who says there was one?"

"A wild guess," he replied.

He'd learned a little bit about the *Englishers* during his *Rumspringa*, and they weren't so different at heart. Amish young people sometimes went a little wild, and they always had a reason. When a man left his community to find a wife elsewhere, he also had a reason that went deeper than simply looking for girls he didn't know so well. And when an *Englisher* girl raised on a farm went to the city to work with people the most desperate for help, he was willing to guess that she had one, too. Everyone seemed driven by something.

"My sister died when I was fifteen," Grace said after a beat of silence. "So that was the traumatic event, I suppose. And after that, I wanted to be in a position to help people—to save a few lives."

"Your sister didn't have to die," Ben concluded.

"No, she didn't." Grace lifted her chin and met his gaze. "There is a lot of pain in this world, and not enough people helping to soothe it. I want to be on the right side."

She was brave. Most people, when faced with the pain of the world, would go back to where they were safe. That's what he'd done. The *Englisher* life might look free and easy from the outside, but there were pressures they endured that the Amish couldn't even guess about.

The wind rattled the door again, and they both turned toward it.

"Let's get back inside the house," he said. He grabbed a wedge of wood from above the door, and when they went outside again and shut the door, he pushed the wedge under the door to hold it shut.

"You're prepared," Grace said, raising her voice above the wind.

"I try," he replied.

He looked toward the barn, and he spotted his father heading in their direction. All would be well. Now it was time to hunker down in the warmth of the house and wait out the storm.

The snow was already ankle-deep, and as they headed toward the house, he saw the drifts rising up the side of Grace's car like a slow white wave. It was like the storm was intent on swallowing it whole.

But inside the house, the lantern glowed cheerily, and a trail of smoke rose up from the chimney and then was blasted apart by the wind, adding the scent of wood smoke to the winter air.

Grace tugged the coat closer and tucked her chin into its depths as Ben opened the door. She might have been farm-raised, but she wasn't dressed for the weather in those dust-streaked dress pants, and he felt an undeniable urge to protect her. He put his hand on her back to nudge her inside ahead of him.

Sometimes the hardest thing to do in life was to wait, and storms seemed to be sent to teach them just that. Until this storm stopped, they had no other choice than to be patient.

Chapter Three

That evening, after the supper dishes were washed and put away, Grace stood with Iris in her kerosene-lamp-lit bedroom. It was in the far corner of the house, away from the kitchen, and over top of the laundry room. Outside the window, all was black, except for some swirling snow nearest the glass.

Ben had carried the cradle upstairs and placed it between the two twin beds in the room, and the baby was fast asleep, sucking on a pacifier. She was swaddled in a soft, warm blanket, and Grace looked down at her tenderly.

"My sister used to share this room with me," Iris said. "And we kept the bed in here in case someone visits. We don't have a guest room right now."

Iris pulled a nightgown out of her drawer and handed it over.

"You'll need a dress in the morning, too," Iris said. "Amish dresses are very comfortable, you know. I don't know how you wear pants like that. Don't they feel funny on your legs?"

"Pants are warmer," Grace said.

And yes, they did feel funny on her legs, even now. But she liked the added warmth that skirts didn't provide in the winter months.

Iris met her gaze, but she didn't look convinced. "I'll get you an apron, too, and—"

"No, no—"

"It would be fun to dress you up like an Amish woman. You'd look Amish! You might like it. The thing with our cape dresses is that they are modest, but they're also flattering on every figure. They adjust, you see—" Iris held out one of her dresses to demonstrate. "You sew your own dress so that you can make it the right size, and then if you gain a little weight or lose it, everything adjusts." Iris smiled brightly. "We Amish aren't supposed to be vain, but we like looking nice, too."

Grace dropped her gaze. This was starting to feel like a lie, not letting this family know that she wasn't quite so lost in the Amish culture as they might think.

"Are you sure you don't want a white apron like I wear? It will just pull it all together—complete the look," Iris said.

That was the problem. She didn't want to complete the Amish look. She didn't want to step back into an Amish life when she'd worked this hard to move forward into an English one. The very last thing she wanted was to don Amish clothes again. The dress was unavoidable, but she wouldn't wear the other Amish items.

"Iris, I'm—" Grace swallowed. "I was raised Amish."

Iris froze, and then her eyes widened. "Really?"

"*Yah*, I know what the clothing means to an Amish woman, and it's no game for me," she said, switching to Pennsylvania Dutch. "I won't disrespect them, and I hope you understand that I'm trying to be as respectful as possible."

"Why aren't you Amish anymore?" Iris breathed.

"It's…complicated. I changed my mind about some things," Grace said. "I don't really want to get into it. And believe me, I had no intention of being a burden on your family. I'm sorry."

She wasn't sure what else to say, and for a moment, Iris was silent. Then she held out the nightgown wordlessly.

Grace accepted the flannel nightgown. "Thank you. I appreciate it."

Grace slipped out of her clothes and into the thick, warm nightgown. Grace paused at the window again. She couldn't see her car, and that made her feel a little adrift.

"You might change your mind, you know," Iris said. "You might come back to the faith."

Grace didn't want to argue or make this any more awkward than it already was, so she just smiled. "*Gott* knows."

Maybe the snow would stop overnight, and she'd be on her way to the city tomorrow morning. Hopefully in the morning, she'd just get back into her business suit, and she could leave this farm with its too-familiar ways far behind her and get back to her apartment, her job and her regular *Englisher* life, where she never quite seemed to figure out the subtleties that made sense to everyone else.

It was better than being stuck in an Amish home where she understood all too well…

Iris put a hand against her forehead. She heaved a sigh and moved toward her bed.

"I think I'll sleep," she said. "For some reason, I'm really tired tonight. I feel like I might be catching something."

"I hope not," Grace said.

"Sleep always helps. I'll be fine," Iris replied.

Sleep helped a multitude of problems, and it also cleared minds. She'd best get to bed, too. The baby would be up for another bottle, no doubt, so she'd need all the rest she could get.

Grace pulled back the covers and slid into a crisp, clean bed. The house was cooling, and outside the window, the wind moaned, snow swirling past the glass. Iris turned off the lamp, and the room sank into darkness. There was a Bible on top of the chest of drawers between them, and if Grace were at home, she'd read a passage before sleeping. In the dark, she wouldn't be able to.

But there was her phone… She had a downloaded version she had installed on it, and while she normally used her electronic version when she was in a waiting room or something, tonight she might not have much choice. She pulled out her cell phone, and the verse of the day popped up. It must have updated before she lost internet. It was the twenty-third Psalm—Tabitha's favorite. Before she passed away, when she was bedridden and ever so thin, she used to ask Grace to read it to her. Grace would go over those familiar words, and Tabitha would let out a deep sigh. That Psalm comforted her sister, and it had comforted Grace, too.

> The Lord is my shepherd; I shall not want. He maketh me to lie down in green pastures: he leadeth me beside the still waters. He restoreth my soul…

As Grace's eyes moved over the familiar verse in the soft glow of her phone's screen, a warning popped up for low battery. She sighed and turned off the phone, holding down the button until it shut off completely. She'd best save what little battery was left.

The truth was, Grace needed some restoration of her soul, too. She'd been so angry that her community wouldn't listen to her about more doctor's visits, about regular checkups and following the public health recommendations of their state. She was only a teenaged girl. She had no voice for things like that. After her sister's death, she'd known she couldn't just go back to following the rules again, *trusting* the rules again. And she'd hoped to find that healing in her heart out there with the *Englishers*—the people who weren't curtailed by the *Ordnung*, or by tradition or by a family's way of doing things. While she'd learned a lot in her time at college and in her career, the healing she'd been longing for hadn't been so easily won.

The *Englishers* weren't any more at peace than she was.

And lying on that pillow, the baby slumbering in the cradle between them, Grace looked across the dim room to where Iris lay in her bed. Iris coughed a couple of times and pulled her blankets up closer around her head. Sharing an Amish bedroom with another young woman felt most familiar of all for Grace, and an overwhelming sense of loneliness for her sister washed over her.

Grace fell asleep at long last, and she was awoken early the next morning by Taylor's cry. Grace pushed her covers back and shivered in the cold. The clock on the dresser showed four o'clock, which was about the right time for an Amish household to be waking up. She picked the baby up and cuddled her close. Once she was in Grace's arms, she stopped crying, but Taylor's little mouth was searching for milk, and her diaper was in need of a change. Grace looked hopefully toward the window. Snow was still coming down, although the wind had died.

"She's up, is she?" Iris murmured in Dutch.

Iris pushed herself out of bed and shivered, her teeth chattering.

"Are you okay?" Grace asked.

"I don't feel well, actually," Iris said.

Grace reached out and touched Iris's forehead. Her head was hot, and her eyes looked glassy. Iris coughed and shivered again.

"Stay in bed," Grace said. "I'll be okay. Between Ben and your father, we'll sort things out."

Grace changed the baby's diaper and laid her back down in the cradle, then pulled on the dress that Iris had given her last night and layered a cardigan on top of it. Taylor cried piteously until Grace scooped her up again. Iris rose anyway and pulled on a dress of her own.

"I'll be fine," Grace insisted.

"I have to start the stove," Iris said, and she coughed into her elbow. She didn't reach for her *kapp* or apron, though, and she padded out of the bedroom, her hair falling loose around her shoulders. Grace followed with the baby in her arms. Ben's bedroom door opened, and he came out fully dressed.

"Your sister isn't feeling well," Grace said.

"Are you sick, Iris?" Ben asked in Dutch.

"*Yah*, but you all need your breakfast," Iris said.

"We'll be fine, Iris," Ben said. "Sleep in. Maybe you'll feel better later."

Iris nodded and cast Grace an uncertain look. "You can probably handle breakfast?"

"I can cook!" Grace replied. She knew what Iris was asking: How out of practice was she? "I'm sure I can put together a breakfast. Go rest."

Iris disappeared back into the bedroom, and Grace followed Ben down the stairs. The baby started to cry again, and when Ben touched the baby's cheek, Taylor calmed slightly.

"Do you want to try holding her?" Grace asked.

Ben eased the baby out of her arms, and as soon as Taylor was snuggled against his chest, she quieted down.

"I'll get the bottle started," Grace said. "She's pretty hungry. She slept all night."

Ordinarily Grace would warm it first, but the stove wasn't lit yet, and it would take too long. Grace shook up a bottle of formula and handed it over to Ben. He popped it into Taylor's mouth, and she started to slurp back her milk without complaint.

"There…" Grace smiled down at the baby. "Better?"

Taylor's cheeks were wet with tears, and her eyelashes stuck together.

"She likes you, doesn't she?" Grace said quietly.

"*Yah*, she seems to," Ben agreed. "It's not very convenient, though. I need to start the fire in the stove and—"

"I can do it," Grace said. "Like I said, I can start breakfast. Where's the wood?"

Ben nodded at a pile next to the door. Grace went and fetched some, then opened the stove and started scooping out the ashes from yesterday's cooking. She brushed it clean into the ash bucket and then started arranging the wood for a new fire. When she looked up, she found Ben's gaze locked on her.

"You know your way around a woodstove," he said.

Grace licked her lips. "*Yah*, I'll take care of things here."

She'd said the words in Dutch, and Ben's eyes widened. "You… You're Amish?"

She brushed her hands off and rose to her feet. "I *was* Amish. I'm not anymore. I left my community during my *Rumspringa*, and…"

"You're Amish enough to cook on a wood-stove," he said.

"Some things you learn and you don't forget," she said.

Ben nodded, his expression grim, and she felt the silent accusation in his stare. It was a lot like his sister's silent judgment from last night.

"I didn't mean to lie," she said softly.

"No?" His jaw flexed.

"You all assumed I was English, and I am," she said. "For the most part. For all it matters for my future! But I was raised Amish, and... I thought I'd be on my way home by now. There was no need to get into my history."

He chewed the side of his cheek, and for a moment, he seemed to be weighing her words. Then he let out a pent-up breath.

"That's understandable," he said. "You were only supposed to be here long enough to pick up the baby."

"Exactly." So he understood. She smiled at him hesitantly.

"So you weren't just raised on a farm," he said. "You were raised on an Amish farm."

"Yah."

"We thought you couldn't understand Dutch."

Grace felt her cheeks heat. She'd kept her

secrets and listened in on theirs. It hadn't been fair.

"I'm sorry about that," she said. "I wasn't here to make you uncomfortable with my personal history. That would be very unprofessional of me."

Ben was silent for a moment. "It's a little embarrassing. For me, at least."

"Your family loves you, and they tease you," Grace said. "That's all I overheard. I promise."

Hannes's footsteps came creaking slowly down the stairs. Grace bent down to light the match and let the first tinder catch fire. It crackled and started to burn, so she opened the vent and shut the stove door to let it get started.

Hannes carried the cradle, and he put it down beside the kitchen table with a sigh. He looked at Grace in surprise.

"Is my son teaching you to cook like an Amish woman?" Hannes asked good-naturedly.

Grace exchanged a look with Ben.

"Not exactly," Ben said.

Hannes raised his eyebrows but didn't push the issue. He went to the kitchen window and shaded his eyes to look outside.

"Still snowing," he murmured.

"Can you handle breakfast, then?" Ben asked, his voice low.

Grace nodded. "You two go on and do your chores. When you get back, you'll eat."

Taylor finished her bottle then, and Ben tipped her upright. Grace grabbed a towel and put it over her shoulder, then reached for the baby to burp her.

"Let's get out there and check on the herd," Hannes said.

Ben and Hannes headed into the mudroom. Grace tapped Taylor's back gently as she listened to the men's boots thump against the floor, and then the side door opened. A rush of cold air came into the house. Grace moved closer to the stove with the baby.

Whatever sense of anonymity she'd enjoyed so far was officially over. They knew her secret, and she doubted the Hochstetler family was going to approve.

"She's Amish?" Hannes straightened from checking the cow's bandaged leg. Ben crossed his arms over his chest.

The barn was warm enough, the scent of hay and cattle permeating the air. The outside door rattled as a gust of wind battered it, and his father shook his head slowly.

"I'm normally better at seeing these things," Hannes said. "I can't believe I didn't guess."

"I mean, she isn't practicing, but she was raised on an Amish farm, and she can cook on a woodstove and knows what to do for chickens during a storm," Ben said. "We should be thankful for that much."

"That's a help," Hannes said. "Less mollycoddling of a visitor and more working together to get through this."

Hannes nodded a couple of times, seeming happy with this turn of events. He reached for a bale of hay and forked some into a feeder for the goats.

"Which means she understands Dutch," Ben said pointedly.

Hannes stopped work, and his face pinked.

"I'm sorry about that." His father winced. "We honestly thought she couldn't! What's the worst that she heard?"

"That you think I can't attract a woman, for one," Ben said irritably.

"Oh, no harm done there," his father said, and turned back to forking hay again. "She isn't someone for you. We didn't say anything about Charity, did we?"

"No."

"Not so bad, then." Hannes dropped the

pitchfork to the ground with a *clang*. "We'll be fine."

Not so bad… It was for Ben. She might not have been a romantic option, but he was a man with some dignity, after all, and a man's family's opinion mattered. They were teasing…and she seemed to know that, but it didn't reduce his irritation any.

Still, maybe he should be thankful that they hadn't talked about anything more sensitive. Everyone had something they wanted to keep private, and he was no exception to that.

Ben turned back to mucking out some stalls, shoveling soiled hay into a wheelbarrow, the sound of metal against concrete scraping in a comfortable rhythm. Dust motes danced in the light of the kerosene lamp, and as he worked, this new information settled into his head. Grace wasn't an *Englisher*… It did change how he saw her. She wasn't someone new to their way of life. And she certainly wasn't helpless.

But more than that, she was an Amish woman who had *left*. Permanently and by her own choice.

Like Charity had.

The Amish life was one of hard work, dedication and determination, but it was also satisfying. When he worked for something, he felt like he learned more about life and *Gott*. When he raised animals, he gained compassion. When he tilled the soil, he learned patience. And when he looked up at the sky, he felt a connection to *Gott*.

He'd asked Charity to go back home with him. They could get baptized, get married... It was time to stop their rebellious adventure and return to some young adult responsibilities. But Charity's experience with the *Englishers* had been different. She saw a future for herself in the city.

"I don't want to keep a garden, clean a house, cook food and get up at four in the morning every day for the rest of my life!" Charity had said. "I want to have some fun! I want to get in a car and drive somewhere. I want my driver's license..."

So when Ben came home again to Redemption, his family, and the Amish life just before his eighteenth birthday, he'd had to face Charity's family and explain that she wasn't coming back, and that he was so sorry for what he'd done.

He'd had to tell her father, man to man, that after luring her away from the safety of their community, he'd left her in Pittsburgh. A *Rumspringa* wasn't normally that rebellious. It was his fault, and he had to own it.

Her family had been more than angry. They'd been heartbroken. Anger could be mollified. Heartbreak just went on and on.

So when Ben thought about Grace now, he was thinking one thing only—what kept her from going home? He didn't think that made her a bad woman, exactly, but it did mean that she shared something important in common with Charity. And if he could figure that out, then maybe he could forgive himself for having taken Charity with him to Pittsburgh to begin with. Maybe, just maybe, it wasn't entirely his fault.

He finished filling the wheelbarrow and lifted it by the handles, steering it out toward the back to where they dumped the soiled hay. It would be used for fertilizer in the spring. Nothing wasted.

Except for his time in Pittsburgh. That had been a waste. He needed a fresh start somewhere no one knew his biggest failure.

If *Gott* could forgive the worst sinners, then maybe *Gott* could do the same for him and grant him another chance to prove to *Gott* above, to his community, to his family and to himself that he would stay true to the narrow path for the rest of his life.

He brought the wheelbarrow back into the

welcome warmth of the barn and headed over to the next stall.

The worst mistakes a man could make weren't the ones that hurt him; they were the mistakes that hurt others.

Chapter Four

Grace looked down into Taylor's round face. The baby's eyes kept searching, and she opened her mouth in a plaintive cry. Grace had a lot of experience with babies from growing up in a big family, and one lesson she'd learned early was the cry of a baby who wanted her mother... Grace's heart squeezed.

"I know, little one," Grace crooned. "Me, too."

Grace missed her mother as well, but she'd never have the same easy relationship with her that she'd enjoyed growing up. Grace's mother was too deeply disappointed for that. There weren't any long talks anymore, no more smiles of pride when her mother looked over her baking or her gardening.

Because her mother was no longer proud of what Grace had become. Grace was now the morality tale to tell her younger siblings, the example of a girl gone bad.

Grace had left her home community at the age of seventeen, and she'd only returned a handful of times to see her parents. There had been arguments, frustration and stubbornness on both sides. It was just too hard to fight about the same things over and over again. It was too hard to see her parents cry when she left—their hearts so wrung out with frustration and grief that they hadn't been able to hold it in any longer.

So she stayed away for long stretches of time... And she felt guilty for doing so. Grace missed her family. She missed her younger brothers and sisters, her cousins and her extended family. Her upbringing had been a loving one, but her parents couldn't bridge the gap of Grace having gone English. None of them could. Her family thought she'd left her salvation behind.

Grace thought she'd found it.

Taylor started to settle as the heat from the woodstove filled the kitchen. When she stopped crying, Grace wrapped another blanket around her, laid her in the cradle, and then pulled the cradle closer to the stove.

"We'll cook together, sweetie," Grace said. "I'm going to feed people, apparently."

She used to do this when her youngest brother was a baby and her mother had been sick with a particularly bad flu. As long as she could talk to him and rock his cradle with the warmth of the stove keeping him cozy, all had been well. Here was hoping the same thing would work with Taylor, because those men were going to come back in hungry.

She opened a few cupboards and found a pot, which she half filled with water and put on the stovetop. She'd make oatmeal and stir in some cinnamon, nutmeg and sugar. She found the oatmeal in another cupboard, and she eyed the amount as she poured it into the pot. Letting the oatmeal and water come to a boil together made it creamier.

But oatmeal alone wouldn't feed hungry men who'd been out in a storm. She found some bacon in the icebox to fry up and some fresh bread in the bread box on the counter. She could make some butter and bacon sandwiches for the men to carry with them when they went back outside. Funny how it was all coming back to her.

"You need to be farther away from the stove if I'm frying bacon," Grace said. She pulled the heavy cradle to a safe distance, then smiled over at the baby. "I'm still right here, Taylor."

When the fire in the stove started to burn down, Grace opened it again and pushed a few more sticks of wood inside.

"Do you miss it?"

Grace startled and turned to see Iris at the bottom of the stairs, a woolen blanket wrapped around her shoulders. She sniffled into a tissue.

"Come to the stove," Grace said. "Heat will help. I'll make you tea."

Iris came closer and pulled a kitchen chair up to sit on. Grace looked around for the mugs.

"That cupboard—" Iris started to stand.

"I've got it," Grace said. She grabbed a mug and a canister of tea and set to work making a hot cup for Iris. When she handed it over, Iris smiled her thanks and blew on it.

"Well?" Iris asked. "Do you miss this?"

"Cooking?" Grace wiped a dribble of tea from the counter with a cloth. "I cook in the city, too."

"You know what I mean," Iris replied, and she took a sip.

Grace did know what she'd meant. "I don't know," she admitted. "Maybe a little bit. It's coming back. It feels good to take care of something like a meal and be useful in the old ways."

"Do you have anyone to take care of in your English home?" Iris asked.

Grace dropped her gaze. "Not really. I have my aunt over for dinner sometimes, but it's not the same."

"It's different to be needed, I suppose," Iris said.

"I am needed in my job," Grace said. "I might not have a family at home waiting on my cooking, but I do have people in the community who need me very much."

"Like who?" Iris asked. It was an honest question.

"Well, there are struggling families that need our services," Grace said. "Like single mothers who are trying to make ends meet, and they need help finding government aid. Then there are elderly people who live alone, and sometimes people try to take advantage of them. So we check in and make sure they're okay, too."

"What about their families?" Iris asked. "Isn't anyone taking care of them?"

"Not everyone has a family." Grace pulled the bacon out of the pan and put it on a plate. "Sometimes, people have fractured relationships, and sometimes they didn't have children, and they weren't close to their nieces and nephews...and somehow, they end up by themselves in their old age."

"What about their churches?" Iris asked.

"The ones who have churches have community," Grace admitted. "There are people to look in on them and bring them food or take them to the service. But not everyone has a church, either..."

Some people ended up on their own, despite all their best efforts to build that family connection they craved, and Grace had to admit she was afraid of being in that exact position.

"And sometimes," Grace went on, softening her tone, "there is a situation like this one where a baby is abandoned, and we have to step in and help find that little one a safe home."

"It's sad to think of people being so alone," Iris said.

"Which is why I'm needed," Grace replied.

There was a hiss as oatmeal boiled over onto the black stovetop, and the smell of burning oatmeal suddenly filled the air. Grace sighed and grabbed a towel to pull the lid off the pot. She snatched up a wooden spoon and plunged it inside to stir, only to feel a burned layer on the bottom of the pot.

"Oh...for crying out loud," she muttered.

She'd stoked up the stove and burned the oatmeal in the process. "It's ruined."

Outside the window, she saw the gray shape of the men returning through the snow. There was no time to make another batch.

"Let me help you," Iris said, and she pulled the blanket closer around her shoulders, then reached for an oven mitt. She moved the pot over to the cool side of the stove, and Grace sent the younger woman a grateful smile.

"I was supposed to let you rest," Grace said.

Iris shrugged. "It's okay." She coughed into the blanket and touched her forehead again. "We have some applesauce we can put on top of the oatmeal, too. It'll mask the taste a little bit."

"I feel bad," Grace said.

"You act like you're the first one to burn a pot of oatmeal." Iris chuckled, and she coughed again.

"I've got the rest," Grace assured her, and she started laying strips of bacon into the pan with a sizzle.

When Taylor started to fuss again, Iris began to rock the cradle with her foot, leaving Grace to focus on the cooking. The oatmeal would taste burned, regardless, but the bacon turned out well, and by the time the men came stamping into the mudroom, she was buttering bread and putting crisp strips of bacon between thick slices.

Ben came into the kitchen first, and he looked behind him into the mudroom.

"*Daet*, let's get you some tea," Ben said.

Hannes appeared in the doorway looking pale and shivering. He was sick, too, and Grace immediately began filling another mug of tea for the older man. He pulled a chair up closer to the stove and held his hands out toward it.

"Here," Grace said. "Some extra sugar in the tea helps, too."

Hannes accepted the mug with a nod of thanks.

"I'll be fine," he said, and he pulled out a handkerchief and sneezed into it. "It's just a cold."

"A rather bad one," Grace said.

Hannes smiled faintly. "I'm not knocked over as easily as that."

"Let me get some food onto the table," Grace said, and she looked over at the pot of burned oatmeal uncertainly.

"I'll give you a hand," Ben said.

Ben set the table while Grace finished with the bacon sandwiches, and she eyed the big man warily as he lifted the lid on the pot of oatmeal. He froze for a moment, and she could see when the smell hit him, because he seemed to physically repress a reaction.

"Mmm," he said, but his tone lacked enthusiasm. "Oatmeal."

"It burned," Grace said. "I'm sorry! I'm not as good with woodstoves as I used to be. I stoked up the fire, and…"

Ben looked over at her. "No, it's okay. Thank you."

"Your sister suggested putting some applesauce on top of it," Grace said.

"*Yah*, that might help," he replied, then cast her an apologetic look. "I mean, that might taste good."

"You can just say it," Grace replied. "It's burned."

"It's breakfast," Ben said and grinned. "Let's eat."

Ben went into the other room and came back with another woolen blanket that he put around his father's shoulders.

"I'm not as sick as that," Hannes said.

"Your teeth are just about chattering, *Daet*," Ben said.

Hannes took another sip of hot tea. "We'll bring a couple of thermoses out with us. That'll give me a little bit of warmth when I need it."

Ben looked at his father, and his brow creased. Then he glanced over at Grace. Was he thinking what she was—that Hannes had no business going back out into that storm? And Iris certainly shouldn't be going outside in her condition, either. It might be "just a cold," but it would turn into something a lot worse if they didn't take care of themselves now.

They all moved to the table, and Grace took the seat next to Ben. They bowed their heads in silence. When Hannes cleared his throat, they all raised them again, and the dishing up began. Iris didn't take much to eat, and when Taylor started to whimper, Grace was the one who got up to hold the baby again. She was surprised when Ben followed her over to the cradle.

"Grace, how comfortable do you feel around cattle?" Ben asked.

"It's been a while, but I can follow instructions," she replied.

"Because my *daet* is going to claim he's fine, but I'm worried about how he's feeling. I know it's a lot to ask, but would you mind coming outside with me to do chores? I think between Iris and my *daet*, they can take care of the baby, as long as they all stay warm and have some hot tea handy."

"Yah," she agreed with a nod. "I'd be happy to—"

She paused, looking down at the cotton dress she wore. Even with woolen tights, it would be cold out there.

"Ben, just one thing," she said. "I can't do this in a dress only."

"What?" He looked startled.

"I've been away for a long time, and I wear pants out in the cold now. I'll help you, but you've got to lend me some of your trousers."

"My pants?" He rubbed a hand over his chin.

"Actually, your *daet*'s pants might be a better fit." She eyed him hopefully. "He's shorter than you."

Ben started to laugh. "Well, if those are your terms, I don't think I can very well turn them down, can I?"

"Thank you," she said with a smile. "I appreciate it. I don't think I'm quite as farm strong as I used to be."

"I'll explain the situation to my *daet*," he said, but humor still sparkled in his eyes. "And hopefully he sees the funny side of this."

Grace silently agreed—hopefully the older man would see the humor of a visiting social services agent wearing an Amish man's attire, because while she wanted to help, she highly doubted she'd be able to pitch in for very long without some proper layers to keep her warm.

She wasn't Amish anymore, and that applied to her endurance, as well. But she was willing to do her best.

While Grace cleared the table, Ben watched her moving about the kitchen and he couldn't help but admire how pretty she was. Her hair swung in a ponytail as if she were someone's little sister at home with her family. There was something about her—so proper and yet so English at the same time. He'd sensed before that she seemed to fit into an Amish kitchen, and now he understood why—she'd been raised in one.

Watching Grace as she moved through the kitchen, a pile of plates in her hands, he couldn't help but acknowledge that Grace was no little sister, and her glossy waves did catch his eye.

Everyone said he needed a wife, and he'd always put them off by saying he didn't need just any wife—he needed the right wife. He'd seen his friends get married and go through the upheaval of the first year or two, and the thing that made all that adjustment worth it was marrying a girl they loved. He needed that. A nice woman from a nice family wouldn't be enough…and maybe that was because he'd need her to love him that much to make it worth the effort on her side, too. He'd been told over and over again he had a lot to learn about women. His honesty seemed to be the issue, and maybe he needed a woman who didn't mind his clear opinion. It would be exactly what she wanted to hear.

"Stop staring," Hannes said, nudging Ben's arm with his elbow.

Had he been staring? Ben felt his face heat. "Sorry. I didn't mean to."

His father coughed again, and he pulled the blanket closer around himself.

"Look, *Daet*, you're not feeling well, and it's really brisk out there today," Ben said.

"I'm fine. I'm fine," Hannes said. "This is a cold. Colds happen."

"You're not fine. If this is just a cold, it's a bad one, and if you push this, you could end up with pneumonia, like old Jake Miller did," Ben retorted. His father wasn't exactly young anymore.

"Jake Miller worked through three months of a cold winter with a terrible cough," Hannes said. "This is one day."

"Jake Miller died," Ben countered.

"It's only one day," Hannes replied firmly. "I'm fine!"

"We've agreed that you are not fine," Ben said.

"Who is we?" Hannes demanded.

"Grace and I."

His father raised an eyebrow. "Ah. I do hope this new team mentality with an *Englisher* woman doesn't start crossing any lines."

"*Daet*, stop being dramatic," Ben said. "Stay inside, help Iris take care of that *bobbily*, and let me and Grace get the chores done. When the storm passes, Grace will be gone, but until it does, there are chores to tend to, and I'd really rather not carry you back to the house over my shoulder."

"And I'm the one being dramatic now?" Hannes muttered.

Ben glanced up to find Grace watching them over her shoulder as she ran the water in the sink to wash dishes. Was it wrong of him to be looking forward to doing a few chores with her? She wasn't entirely English, and she intrigued him. Besides, she might have a few of the insights that he needed, and what better way to dig them up than working together?

Hannes erupted into a coughing fit. Ben sent up a silent prayer of thanks, at least for the timing of it, because when Hannes finally caught his breath again, he had no argument left in him.

"All right, I'll stay in today," Hannes said. "I'll drink tea with ginger and be ready to work again tomorrow."

"Maybe it's good timing to have Grace here, after all," Ben said with a nod.

"It normally isn't considered polite to put a female guest to work with cattle," Hannes said.

"It's a storm," Ben said. "We do what we have to."

Hannes shivered. "I think I'll go closer to the stove."

"She also needs to borrow a pair of pants," Ben said, and his father looked back at him.

"What?" Hannes's already pale face blanched further.

"She's cold, *Daet*, and she's English now. She's not used to working outside in a dress, and she only has the outfit she came in, so if I want to ask her to help me with the cattle, then I need to provide her with pants."

"I'm not even sure it's proper!" Hannes said, staring at Ben, aghast.

"Yours are closer to her size than mine are," Ben pressed on, undaunted.

"A woman in pants," Hannes said, shaking his head.

"Unless it includes you in a dress, an *Englisher* woman in pants is less of a scandal than you think," Ben replied. "And she's been English since she was a teenager. Can I go find a pair for her, then?"

"If there's no other way," Hannes said, spreading his hands. "And you do *not* have permission to use mine. I'd rather go back out and do the chores myself than let that happen. We have a pair of pants from when young Vernon came to help with the calving, don't we? You could try those."

Ben shot his father a grin. "We do! I know where they are, too. Here's hoping they fit well enough."

The baby started to cry then, and across the room, Grace went over to pick her up. Ben watched her for a moment as she shushed the baby, cuddling her close. She swung back and forth, her cheek against the infant's head, but Taylor continued to cry her desperate wail.

"Bring the *bobbily* to me," Hannes said, pulling his chair closer to the stove.

Grace looked up, and she crossed the kitchen toward Hannes.

"I've been told you two have decided to keep me indoors," Hannes added.

"You don't look well," Grace said earnestly over the baby's cries, and she slid the baby into his arms. Hannes settled the baby into the crook of his arm in that practiced way of his, angling the baby's toes toward the heat and her downy head away from it.

Ben cleared his throat and nodded toward the stairs. "Let me get you some clothes, then, *yah*?"

"Thank you," Grace replied.

Ben found that pair of fleece-lined pants from his nephew Vernon's visit the year before, and he dug out a sweater from his sister's closet and a T-shirt from his own. It would be a strange outfit to be sure, but it would do for now to keep her warm underneath a borrowed winter coat.

Grace accepted the clothes with a smile of thanks, but she frowned at the T-shirt.

"I'm not dressing all the way…like a man," she said. "I need the pants for under the dress."

The realization came with a flood of relief, and Ben laughed uncomfortably.

"I thought—" He shook his head. "I just thought you wanted to dress more comfortably in an *Englisher* way, and that meant—"

Grace raised her eyebrows. "And you were willing to accommodate me, even so. Ben, you are very kind. But no, I won't entirely scandalize your home today. I won't wear a *kapp* and apron, but I also won't march around dressed like a man."

"Will you need suspenders?" Ben asked, holding up a pair. He was teasing her now, and Grace's face colored.

"You're very funny," she said, rolling her eyes. "But no, thank you."

Grace slipped into Iris's bedroom, and Ben went back downstairs. Hannes sat by the stove, the baby quiet in his arms. He rhythmically patted her diaper and hummed a hymn, and as Ben came back into the kitchen, his father's eyes followed him. Ben washed the dishes while his sister made another pot of tea.

"You know that she was raised Amish, right?" Iris said.

"*Yah*, I learned that this morning," Ben said. "But we should be glad that she was, because burned or not, she could make breakfast for us."

"I agree," Iris said. "I also think you like her."

"She's helping us, Iris," he said. "And I'm grateful. And she can also understand Pennsylvania Dutch, so keep your voice down, would you?"

"She's pretty, too," Iris countered, wiping

her nose with a tissue and shooting him a grin. "And single. I asked."

So had he, but he wouldn't tell his sister that. "Iris, she's English now."

"Right now she's English, yes," Iris said. "But who knows about the future?"

Ben chuckled. "Even sick and miserable, you're trying to get me married. I think we should just focus on your wedding, don't you think?"

Grace's footsteps sounded on the stairs. He turned to see her coming down—the pants worn underneath the Amish dress, and the sweater pulled on top. It looked comical but not quite so scandalous as he'd feared.

"Grace, I feel bad sending you out into that storm," Hannes said. "I'm happy to pass the baby over to you, and—"

"I'm volunteering," Grace said, reaching the bottom of the stairs. "It will be nice to do some farm work for a change. I've been getting soft sitting behind a desk."

Soft... It was an apt word to describe her. She had a certain softness about her, but she was also a little wild. It was the exact combination that seemed to be his weakness.

"Take care of her out there, Ben," Iris said.

Ben sent his sister an annoyed look. She was teasing him, and he wasn't in the mood for it. He led the way into the mudroom. Grace already had the boots she'd borrowed earlier, and he passed her his old coat that was far too big for her, but it was better than nothing. Then he fished an extra pair of gloves for her out of a box above the coat hooks. Grace nearly disappeared under all of the layers of too-big outerwear.

"You may have to remind me how to do things, though," she said. "It's been a few years."

She might be Amish-born, and she might be an English woman now with some authority of her own, but standing there in his old winter coat with nothing but her eyes and nose visible above the zipper, he felt a wave of protectiveness for her.

She wasn't being rebellious against the Amish traditions. She just knew what she could do after being away so long…and what she could handle. He couldn't treat her like an Amish woman today.

"It'll be fine," he reassured her. "I won't have you do anything too hard, and I'm not leaving you alone out there, either."

Her eyes crinkled up into a smile. "Good. I expect you to bring me back to this house in one piece."

"That I can guarantee," he said. "Come on, then. The sooner we get out there, the sooner we can come back and warm up."

Chapter Five

The pants fit snugly around her waist, but the dress caught on the fabric of the pants and held her back a little bit. She was warm enough in the layers of sweater and coat, though, and when Ben opened the door, a frigid wind whipped in to meet them. She followed him outside. Wind gusts made closing the door behind them difficult. Grace pulled it hard, and it didn't catch, pushing back open again. Ben reached past Grace to slam the door for her, and she smiled at him, not even sure if he could see much more than her eyes.

The morning was bright enough now that there was no need for a lantern to light the way, and they marched down the snow-covered steps. The blizzard swirled around them, blinding her momentarily to anything but the dark outline of the back of Ben's coat. She hurried after him, her head down.

It had been a long time since she'd done chores on a farm. The last time had been as a teenager, working alongside both her parents during harvest. Every year, they pitched in together, but most of the work left to Grace had been keeping her younger siblings out of the way. Plus, she'd taken over the cooking and cleaning in the house while her *mamm* went out into the fields with her *daet*. Then, in the evenings, when *Mamm* took over with getting the little ones bathed and put to bed, Grace would go out with her *daet* to finish the last of the chores.

"You'll make a good farmer's wife one day," her father used to tell her teasingly. "Just not too early—you hear?"

Back then, her father had honestly worried about her getting married too young to know her own mind, and she'd thought about that after she left. With the *Englishers*, there was no threat of any kind of marriage—wise or reckless. She simply didn't have any man interested enough in her for that. If she'd stayed Amish, would it have been different? Would she have gotten married at nineteen or twenty? Would she have some little ones of her own by now? Or had her *daet* just seen her with the loving eyes of a father who couldn't imagine her being passed over?

The cold air swirled into the hood of her coat, and the icy wind pressed through her dress and pants together. When the wind paused or changed direction briefly, she could see the red barn through the snowfall, but then the snow blocked her vision again.

The wind howled, and when a strong blast stopped her in her tracks, she shut her eyes against the stinging pellets of snow. When she opened them again, she couldn't see a thing. Everything was white, and the back of Ben's coat was gone.

She turned in a circle, her breath coming fast. She couldn't make out anything—not the house, not the barn… Her heart hammered hard in her chest.

"Ben?" she shouted. "Ben!"

Nothing. She froze, waiting for the wind to shift again. It did, and just as her view cleared, she realized she was facing the wrong direction, looking at the house with the light shining in the windows. It hadn't taken much to get her sense of direction muddled, and she felt a surge of panic. Then she felt a hand on her arm, and she turned to see Ben. He grabbed her gloved hand.

"Stay close!" he said.

As if she needed a reminder of that! She felt a rush of relief. His grip on her hand was firm and strong, and she hurried to catch up to his long strides. It felt strange to have a man holding her hand this way—as if he had a right to it. Truth be told, she'd never held a man's hand before…besides her father's hand when she was young.

"Slow down!" she gasped, catching her breath.

"Sorry." His pace slowed, but his grip on her hand didn't relax. He leaned closer to her to be heard over the wind. "Some storm, isn't it?"

"*Yah.* I'm glad I didn't try to drive in it!"

He bent closer. "What?"

"I'm glad I didn't try—" She shook her head. "Nothing!"

They plunged ahead together, and it was easier if she leaned in his direction, allowing herself to be swept along beside him. He was holding her hand to keep them together. She knew that. But her heartbeat sped up at the feel of his strong fingers closed over hers.

The blinding wind closed off their view again, but Ben didn't slow. He kept moving forward, his footsteps sure. She slipped once, her boots sliding out from beneath her. She fell to her knees. He stopped and put a hand under her arm. She struggled to her feet, stepping on the hem of the dress. He tugged it free from her boot, and she straightened.

"You okay?" he asked, leaning toward her so that she could make his face out in the blur of snowfall. His dark eyes were concerned.

"I'm fine!" she said, forcing a smile. Was this what it was like to have a boyfriend or a fiancé? She'd seen other women holding their boyfriends' hands, and she'd wondered what it would feel like to be swept along in a strong man's wake. They pushed forward again.

The wind changed once more, and they were closer to the barn now. They closed the last few yards with their heads bent down against the powerful wind. Ben put a hand out, and she heard it thump against the barn siding. Then he released her and felt along the wooden wall until he got to the door.

"Here!" he called, and he heaved it open.

Grace kept one hand on the side of the barn as she made her way over to where Ben waited for her, and she paused when she got to him, his arm extended to hold the door open.

"Go in," he said, and those dark eyes caught hers. His voice was strong and held command, so she ducked under his arm and into the barn with a sigh of relief. The door banged shut behind them, and for a moment, they stood in silence while her eyes adjusted to the dim interior. The bleat of goats came from the far side of the barn, and Grace sucked in a breath that smelled of animals and hay and brought a wave of girlhood memories with it.

Ben stood next to her, the arm of his coat brushing against hers, and she refused to look at him. Maybe if she'd had an *Englisher* boyfriend before, this wouldn't all feel so intimate. But she never had dated. Romance in the English world was oddly complicated. Or was it something about her that put men off? She'd always thought a man would simply make his intentions known. But it didn't seem to work that way.

Grace stomped the snow off her boots. Ben left her side and shook off his coat. He grabbed a lantern from a shelf, then struck a match to light it. The golden glow was a relief, and Ben hung it on a nail from a rafter.

Ben caught her gaze, and a smile tickled his lips. "Not the best time for a reintroduction to farm life, is it?"

"Well, there wouldn't be any reintroduction without this storm," she said. "I'd be back in Vaughnville right now, enjoying a Starbucks coffee in my office."

"I was in Pittsburgh for a few months, but I never did try Starbucks," he said.

"Why not?" she asked.

"Too expensive. I couldn't afford it," he said. "Besides, it felt…"

"Incredibly English?" she supplied.

"Sort of," he said, nodding in acceptance. "I didn't feel comfortable there. It was too busy, too pricey, and everyone had this different language for things."

"They do," she agreed. "But it's delicious. Cappuccinos, mochas, all those frothy, delicious drinks… I allow myself one per day. I get it on the way in to the office. I stop by a drive-through."

"I didn't have to get the hang of those since I didn't drive," he said.

"What were you doing in Pittsburgh?" she asked.

"I had some friends in the city. Well, friends of friends," he said.

It didn't explain much, and maybe she shouldn't expect him to. It wasn't really her business.

"I drink my coffee black," he added.

"Somehow, that doesn't surprise me." She cast him a grin.

"I think you might be spoiled now." Ben laughed, and he headed across the barn, his voice reverberating back to her. "Starbucks coffee from a drive-through, a city office, living in an apartment… You won't have any calluses at all by now."

She didn't, actually, and she felt her face heat. "I'm not as soft as you think, Ben Hochstetler."

He came back to where she stood, pulled off his gloves and tucked them under his arm.

"Give me your hands," he said.

She held her gloved hands out mutely, and he plucked off one glove and turned her hand over. He ran his rough fingers over her palm, his touch moving lightly down to her fingertips, and every nerve stood on edge.

"As I thought," he said with a teasing smile. "Smooth as calfskin leather. Spoiled."

"I support myself completely," she said, meeting his gaze. "I work almost fifty hours a week, every week, and I'm responsible for my own bills, my own home, my own retirement when I'm too old to keep working in an office—I have to pay for it all, I'll have you know. That's not spoiled."

Ben cocked his head to one side, considering.

"You should find yourself a husband to take care of you," he said. "Then you wouldn't have to worry about the money for when you're old."

"It doesn't always turn out that way," she said. "Even if you get married, life happens. There are always worries. I'm just realistic about mine."

"What's the last bit of manual labor you've done?" he asked.

"I changed the tire of my car," she said.

His eyebrows went up. "That impresses me."

"I'm so glad," she said jokingly. "I'm out here helping, aren't I?"

"Just don't wander off in the storm on me, and we'll be fine," he said, and his laugh echoed through the barn. "Come on!"

He was teasing again, and she rolled her eyes. She'd had an older cousin who used to pester her as a girl, and Ben was reminding her strongly of Josiah. Always teasing, always finding a way to get her to react.

"So tell me about these *Englishers* with their milky coffee," Ben said. He grabbed a pitchfork and handed it to her. "Is that like Coffee Soup?"

"My great-grandmother told me about Coffee Soup," she said. "They used it in the Great Depression."

Coffee Soup was just like it sounded—

strong coffee with cream and a little sugar in a bowl or a mug, and buttered or dry toast dipped into it. It was a breakfast that could stretch…and that could use up dry crusts of bread.

"Starbucks is a little fancier than that," she added.

"Well, yes," he agreed. "But it's the same idea."

"I've figured out how to make my own version," she said. "It's something close. You have to heat the milk and whip it until it's frothy so that you're putting a frothy top to the mug of milky coffee…and I use some nutmeg in mine—it's a whole process."

"Sounds like Fancy Coffee Soup to me," he said.

She laughed. "Are you always this flexible and pleasant?"

"Almost always." He laughed, then nodded toward a cow in a stall. "This cow has a hurt leg. Can you fork some hay into that stall right next to her? I'm going to check the bandage, and then we'll bring her over to the clean stall so I can muck out the one she's in."

"Sure," Grace replied.

They both put their gloves to the side, and Grace started to work. Her muscles weren't used to wielding a heavy pitchfork anymore, but she did her best to hide it from Ben's penetrating gaze.

"Are you really telling me that you make that *Englisher* brew?" Ben asked.

"I'm not only telling you that I make it," Grace replied with a teasing grin. "I'm telling you that you'd like it."

Ben chuckled, the sound low and deep, as he bent to inspect the cow's leg.

Grace continued spreading hay over the cement floor of the new stall, and when she was done, she leaned the pitchfork against the wall. Ben had removed the bandage from the cow's leg, and a swollen joint was visible. The cow wasn't putting any weight on it, either.

"Is it bad?" Grace asked quietly.

"It's not good," Ben said with a sigh. He looked up. "Can you grab me that roll of bandage from the shelf over there?"

Grace looked in the direction he'd nodded, and she spotted a shelf full of various bottles and boxes. She went over, her gaze skimming past the familiar brands. There were ear tags, syringes for giving medication, deworming medicine, peroxide, some general antibiotics, eye spray, hoof repair gum... The thick tensor bandage was in a paper wrapping, and she picked it up and brought it back to the stall.

She bent down next to him, and winced looking at the cow's injured leg.

"How did that happen?" she asked. "Gopher hole?"

"Probably," he replied. "We saw her limping in the pasture, so we brought her back to watch her and make sure it healed up properly."

"My *daet* used to hate those gopher holes," she said. "He'd set all sorts of traps to catch them."

"Hold this, would you?" Ben took the wrapper off the bandage.

Grace reached for the wrapper, and she felt her coat brush the cow's leg. She saw the cow's weight shift forward, and before she had time to react, the cow's hoof struck out. She fell back with a strong shove as Ben's arm shot out across the front of her shoulders.

For a moment, Grace struggled to inhale.

"Maybe we should get you out of the stall." He stood up, then bent and caught her arm, helping her to her feet as he guided her a little farther from the cow.

"Yah…" Grace went out the gate, Ben behind her. He shut it solidly. "I'm out of practice with cattle."

"You are," he said seriously. "If I'd moved

a little slower, she would have caught you in the head."

The image of the potential accident was a daunting one, and she suppressed a shiver.

"But she didn't," Grace replied, brushing some straw off her dress. "I'm fine."

"That scared me. You might like taking care of yourself like an *Englisher*, but while you're here, you're my responsibility, you know."

There was something gentle in his voice when he said it, and she felt a rush of warmth in response.

"I'm in one piece still," she said, pushing back her softer feelings. It wouldn't do her any good to start wishing for something that wasn't hers.

"Let's keep it that way." A smile tugged up one side of his lips, and he turned and went back into the stall. He shut the gate behind him with a decisive *click*.

"Why don't I start the goats' stalls?" Grace suggested.

"Thanks," he said. "I do appreciate the help."

Grace caught his dark gaze following her as she headed toward the goats. She was his responsibility. There was a certain sense of safety and security that she'd left behind when she'd left home. Back then, she'd been her *daet*'s responsibility. He'd provided for her, worried about her, made sure that everything she needed was there. And when she married, it was expected that her husband would do the same—make sure her needs were met financially and otherwise, just as she'd do for him in the home. It was a sheltered feeling that she'd chosen to forget.

Grace blew out a slow breath.

Not that it mattered. She'd be heading home soon enough and giving a full report to her supervisor about her time here. She'd get back to work and her regular routines. Life would carry on. This man was Amish, and she was no longer. Familiar as this life might be, she couldn't allow herself to pretend.

Grace Schweitzer might be Amish-born and Amish-raised, but she'd chosen to be English. She'd left that protective circle behind her.

Ben carefully rewrapped the cow's leg, working quickly. He didn't want to try the animal's patience, but as he worked, he kept an eye on Grace. She pushed a wheelbarrow over to the goats' large corner stall. She opened the gate, then brought it inside and shut the gate behind her. She stood for a moment, watching the goats—three adults and two kids. They were all gentle enough animals, but he was glad to see that her first instinct was to observe them.

Ben still felt a little shaken about that near miss with the cow's hoof. He couldn't tell how he'd moved as quickly as he had—maybe *Gott* had been in that. Regardless, she'd almost had a fatal accident. It only reminded him that she was more English than Amish, and he'd have to keep an eye on her. If his father and sister weren't ill, he'd bring Grace back to the house, but she was in better shape than Hannes or Iris right now. Ordinarily, he'd go to the Lapp farm next door, or to the farm down the road by the Amish phone booth, owned by his *Englisher* friend, Steve. *Englisher* or not, that farmer would lend a hand whenever called upon, and he'd stop and chat by a fence just like an Amish farmer. But the neighbors might as well be a hundred miles away. In this storm, they were just as accessible.

And yet her words clung to his mind. She took care of herself. In every way. Was that competence or simply being very much alone? There was no one to help her, no one to make sure the bills were paid, to worry about the future, to make sure she got safely in for the evening. He knew what the Pittsburgh streets were like at night, and if Vaughnville was similar, she could use a strong man who cared about her safety.

That wasn't his job, was it? He wasn't English, and she wasn't staying here. If she needed that male partner in life, she'd have to sort it out on her own. But what did it say about him that he was still thinking about it?

For the next few minutes, he worked on mucking out the cow's stall, and when he was finished, he ambled over to where she was forking soiled hay into the wheelbarrow. He used a couple of hay hooks to grab a fresh bale from the pile in a corner and carried it over. They still needed the lamplight with the blizzard making everything darker, and he let himself into the stall to help her finish up.

"I could probably take care of the rest of the chores on my own," he said.

"I can help you," she said. "I'm fine, Ben. Really."

"I don't want to have to carry you back to the house, either," he said ruefully. "You've done a lot."

Grace's gaze moved away from his face and up over his shoulder. Ben turned to see what she was looking at, and he sighed.

"That goat," he said. "I still don't know how he gets up there!"

A trapdoor into the loft above was open, and looking down at them through the hole was a baby goat. Ben must have left the trapdoor open the night before, because normally it stayed firmly shut for this very reason. But the mechanics of getting that goat up through the trapdoor? It was still lost on him.

"We can't leave him up there," Ben added. "He'll chew through twine, and leave his droppings all over the place. He has to come down."

"Is that a one-man job?" Grace asked, raising one eyebrow. Was she teasing now? Something almost amused sparkled in her brown eyes.

"No, it's not," he admitted.

"Ben, I'm stuck here as long as this storm is blowing, and it makes me feel better to know that I'm at least pitching in around here," Grace said. "Your *daet* and sister are both ill, and this is where I'm most useful. So let me help!"

Ben rubbed his hand over his chin and eyed her for a moment. He didn't have a lot of choice. What was riskier—bringing his father or sister out here in their condition, or having this mostly English woman help him?

"All right. Now, here's the plan. I'm going up there. I'll catch that kid and hog-tie him, then lower him down to you. You've got to stand on a bale of hay to get high enough."

Grace nodded. "*Yah*, we can do that."

It didn't take too long for Ben to haul a fresh bale to the necessary spot, and then he climbed up into the loft. Chasing down the goat was another story, but once he had him by one leg, he was able to wrangle him into submission amid furious bleats, and then tie his legs together.

The goat writhed and twisted as he carried him over to the opening, and he looked down into Grace's upturned face. Her lips were parted, and her gaze was locked on the goat.

Did she have to be so distractingly pretty?

"All right," Ben said, bending down. He eased the fighting animal down through the opening, and Grace held her hands up to steady him. The goat landed solidly in her arms, and she held on tighter than Ben thought she'd be able to. She squatted down on the hay bale and put the goat down before jumping to the ground. Ben closed the trapdoor firmly, then headed down the ladder, and together they untied the goat and sent it back into the stall with its sibling.

Ben heaved a sigh, then shot her a grin.

"You're tougher than I thought you'd be."

"For you, that's a compliment, isn't it?" she asked with a chuckle.

"*Yah*, of course," he replied. "Why wouldn't it be?"

Grace rolled her eyes. "Your sister might have a point about how smooth you are with the women, you know."

Ben laughed. "Why? What would you rather I say? That you're pretty?"

Color touched her cheeks. "I'm not fishing for compliments."

She didn't need to fish for them. She was incredibly attractive. There was something about the way her eyes sparkled just before the smile touched her lips, and the way her hair shone in the low light of the kerosene lamp. She was slim, but not too slim. She had softness to her, too.

"You are also a very inappropriate choice if I was to set my sights on you," Ben said. He'd meant it jokingly, but it was true, too. "So telling you that I think you're pretty or that I like your hair…that wouldn't be useful to either of us, would it?"

"Instead, you could say that I'm sturdy." There was that sparkle in her eye again. "Or that I'm steady on my feet. You could compliment how much I can lift."

Ben rolled his eyes. "You think I'm that bad, do you?"

"I'm just helping you out," she said with a laugh. "Oh! You could tell me that you like how I don't worry about my looks."

Ben barked out a laugh. "If you listen to my sister, my problem is my honesty. And none of that would be honest. Frankly, you don't lift that much, you aren't that steady on your feet, and as far as sturdiness, goes..." He cocked his head to one side, pretending to consider, then shook his head. "And whether you worry about your looks or not..." He shrugged. "You are pretty."

And there it was—his brutal honesty that seldom did him any good.

"Oh..." She smiled faintly at that. "Well, thank you."

"You must have some *Englishers* trying to court you," he said.

"*Englishers* don't court me," she said. "I don't think they court at all. Not the way Amish do. Amish do things purposefully, and the English seem to stumble into it. I'm not very good at the stumbling part."

"You'd think a woman who knows what she wants is a good thing," Ben said.

"You'd think. You'd also be wrong."

She laughed at her own wry humor. Did the *Englisher* men really not fall over themselves for a girl like her? It was hard to believe.

"You said before that *Englishers* court in cars and go to coffee shops," he said. "Are you telling me there were no Starbucks dates with Coffee Soup with eligible men?"

Her cheeks pinked again, and she turned away. "A few. I never did figure out how to get beyond a couple of coffee dates, though."

Ben crossed his arms. "You and me—we might be more alike than I thought."

"Why's that?" she asked.

"I'm a rather hopeless one to match up, too," he said.

"But we know what your problem is," she said, and she started to laugh. "I can't figure out what I'm doing wrong!"

The thought of Grace longing for connection and love and not managing to find that relationship… It squeezed at his heart a little bit.

"Is there someone you're…hoping for?" he asked. And was there a defendable reason for his mild feeling of jealousy at the thought of it?

"Not really," she said. "I think the kind of man I'm hoping for doesn't exist."

"Why?"

"Because I haven't found him yet," she replied.

Yah, he felt the same way. He'd found a woman who cared for him like he cared for her, and then he'd brought her to the city with him. He'd never found a woman he wanted to court after Charity. Was it guilt, or just the realization that the kind of woman who drew him in wasn't going to be good for him, after all? Sometimes a man could have a certain type that enthralled him, and that type could be all wrong for him.

"Can I ask you something?" He adjusted his hat.

"Yah."

"You went English, and it doesn't sound like it's working for you—romantically speaking, at least. Why do you stay?"

Grace was silent for a moment. "I suppose I haven't given up yet."

"Is the English life really better?" he asked. Because he'd lived English for six months, and he'd experienced the convenience, the entertainment, the fun… He'd still come home.

"Not better," she said. "Just better for me."

He nodded. *Yah*, it was likely the same for Charity. Would she have gone English eventually if he'd never brought her to the city?

Perhaps. She had a rebellious streak in her that had intrigued him, and it was the same with Grace. It was what made her different that drew him in—the English in her.

He had to stop even entertaining the thought of a relationship with her. He needed to go to Shipshewana and court a nice woman. He needed to put his mistakes behind him and move on, but it wouldn't happen in Redemption.

"I'm moving to a new community in a few weeks," Ben said. "Maybe you should try the same thing."

"I have a job," she said. "And it's not so easy to replace it. I have to provide for myself, remember?"

Right. Her job—the reason she was here to begin with. Was this the kind of way that *Englishers* stumbled across each other?

He'd come home to an Amish life for a reason. There was order here, and things made sense. Even his own failure to find a wife made sense. There was no confusion there… and it wasn't because he was too honest, either. It was because he'd had a chance at love and marriage, and he'd ruined it. He'd ruined more than his chance. He'd ruined a person. There were consequences for that.

"Let's finish up in here," he said. "There's still the milking to do."

And then they could get back to the warmth of the stove inside. He looked toward the barn window, and the snow was still coming down.

When would it stop? As long as this storm kept blowing, he was locked inside with a beautiful woman and all his personal regrets.

Chapter Six

Working on the farm was harder than Grace remembered. Back when she was a girl helping her *daet*, he must have done a lot more of the heavy lifting, because her muscles ached by the time they returned to the house. Ben carried a covered tin bucket of milk in one hand, and heavy as it was, he carried the weight easily. She'd tried lifting it in the barn and discovered just how heavy a pail of milk was to her now. She wasn't as strong as she used to be.

Ben walked beside her through the swirling snow, and when their vision was blocked by a blizzard of white, he caught her hand again with his free hand and tugged her solidly against him. There was no request in his strong grip, either. He had milk to get into the house, and they needed to stay together. She felt some heat rise in her cheeks. It wasn't his fault. He was a good-looking man, and his openness with her was making this visit feel more personal than it really was. He wasn't a teasing cousin or a friend of the family. He was a relative stranger, except for a shared background. She had to remind herself of that.

When the wind abated for a moment, he let go of her again, and she almost wished he wouldn't. But the house was ahead.

"Here you are—in one piece as promised," Ben said, stopping in front of the house.

Another swirl of snow blocked their vision, and she felt his gloved hand brush her arm.

"I'm not moving!" she said, loud enough to be heard over the whistling wind.

"Good!" But his hand didn't move away from her arm—his grip strong, but gentle. She shut her eyes. Did he know how this made her long for romance? He'd be embarrassed if he guessed.

The wind died down once more, and she opened her eyes.

"Let's get in there," Ben said.

When they arrived and slammed the door solidly shut behind them, the low moan of the wind felt a little farther away. The warmth of the indoors was a relief. Grace's cheeks stung from the cold, and she passed through the kitchen where Iris sat in front of the stove with the baby in her arms. Grace went upstairs to take the work pants off from underneath her dress. When she came back down, Grace could see Hannes through the doorway to the sitting room with a quilt over him, snoring softly.

"How are you feeling?" Grace asked Iris.

"I'm so tired," the young woman admitted. "Taylor wouldn't let me put her down—crying every time I did. I've changed her diaper and fed her and rocked her... I'm exhausted."

"Here—I'll take the baby," Grace said. "You go on upstairs and sleep. It'll do you good. Do you have any cold medicine here or something to help you with the symptoms?"

Iris placed the baby into Grace's arms. "No, I don't want cold medicine. I'll just let *Gott* and my body sort it out."

"Go on up and rest," Ben said, coming out of the mudroom. "You have a wedding coming up, and you need to be well for it."

Iris nodded. "*Yah*, that's true. I'll go get some rest."

Iris smiled wanly and then headed slowly up the stairs.

"She's really sick," Grace said, turning back to Ben.

"Yah." His gaze was on his sister's back. "We'll have to insist she gets that rest." He glanced over at Grace. "There are leftovers from dinner last night that we can have for lunch, so there's no problem there."

But Grace wasn't worried about eating. In an Amish home, there was always food, and Grace could cook, even if the oatmeal this morning had suggested otherwise.

"My parents wouldn't use cold medicine, either," Grace said. "In fact, I didn't even know there was such a thing until my *Englisher* aunt gave me some after I left home."

"Iris just likes to take care of things naturally," he replied.

Naturally… *Yah*, that had been her parents' view, too. They didn't want extra medication, extra doctor's visits, anything like that. They didn't trust it. If it was English, it was suspect.

"If you get sick, do you take something?" Grace asked.

"I don't get sick that often," he replied.

"But do you?" she pressed.

"I might have some hot tea with ginger and honey," he said. "And I've been known to use a cough drop."

She pressed her lips together, gave the baby a squeeze, then lowered her into the cradle.

Or she attempted to, because Taylor started to cry, and Grace lifted her back up.

She shouldn't be irritated with this family for doing what so many Amish families did. There was no crime in letting a cold run its course, but it reminded her of her home community's tendency to distrust modern medicine, and the old anger was rising, linked to her old grief.

"Grace, what's the matter?" Ben asked.

She looked back over her shoulder. "It's nothing."

"It's something," he countered.

She was here as a social services agent, even if those lines were starting to blur.

She sighed. "It's a bit personal. And I'm here in a professional capacity—"

"Humor me, then," he said, cutting her off. "Let's call this off the clock. Answer me as Grace Schweitzer, the woman."

Did she want to get into this? It was personal...but when she glanced over at Ben, she found his gaze locked on her, his expression bewildered.

"Then let's call it a coffee break, and I'm going to make us some of those lattes I was telling you about." She crossed the kitchen and eased the baby into his arms.

Ben's expression softened as he looked

down at the infant. He did seem to become gentler around the baby. Taylor started to whimper, and Ben began to rock.

Grace went to the stove and opened the door to rekindle the fire inside. Ben didn't say anything else, and she sighed.

"When you go English, you discover some things," she began, her voice low. "Namely, medication that helps with all sorts of issues we didn't need to suffer from. I used to be in bed for two weeks with the flu, and my parents would only give me medication from the drugstore as a last resort. I didn't have to get that sick."

"Are you worried about my sister?" he asked. "If Iris needs it, we'll get her something. Don't worry. But we can't get to a store right now, even if we wanted to."

"It isn't only that," she said. "I mentioned my sister yesterday. I told you that she didn't have to die. By the time she was obviously ill, my parents took her to the doctor. They were loving people. They wanted the best for her. But it was too late by then, because she'd never had a regular checkup! In that community, they were suspicious of *Englisher* doctors because they'd suggest things that went against our way of life. So they shut themselves off to the medical community almost completely, and as a result, my sister's cancer was beyond treatment when they found it!"

Ben was silent.

"And I know the Amish argument that *Gott* doesn't make mistakes. Maybe it was just her time... And maybe it was. But what if it wasn't, Ben?"

"If it wasn't, *Gott* would have healed her," he replied.

That was exactly what her parents had said, and the bishop, the elders, the extended family... They'd all said the same thing. *Gott* gave and *Gott* took away.

"If I put my hand into the oven right now..." Grace said. "If I just shoved my hand into the fire, would it be *Gott*'s will that I was burned? Or would it be because I did something dangerous? The *Ordnung* is there to maintain the community, but we Amish are taught that we have the choice to obey it or disobey it, and the consequences will be ours to bear. By disobeying the *Ordnung*, we put ourselves in danger, right? There are consequences that are outside of *Gott*'s will for our lives?"

"Yah."

"So, we can't put everything on *Gott*! We have choices, too," she went on. "And when we choose to avoid medical interventions or even regular checkups, we put ourselves into a risky situation. But the *Ordnung* doesn't give me guidance on that, does it?"

This was an old argument, one that she'd honed over the years, but being able to state it succinctly didn't change anything. It didn't change minds.

"I'm not sure what to say." Ben shifted uncomfortably.

Neither had her parents, or her uncles and aunts...

"It's okay," she said. "I don't expect you to find some pithy answer that I couldn't dig up in the last seven years. Believe me, I've tried, because I did want to go back home, but I couldn't find an answer that sat right with me. Amish have rules to protect the way of life, to keep change from creeping in and taking away from the benefits of community. But what if those rules, while protecting you from change, don't protect your safety?"

"They protect our souls," Ben said.

"What about our lives?" she asked, shaking her head. "I was taught that the rules, if obeyed to the letter, would keep me safe from all the danger out there. But they didn't protect my sister, did they?"

Grace poked another stick of wood into the belly of the stove, and coals ignited the wood. She was frustrated, and it wasn't right of her to unload all of this onto Ben. He was just an Amish man who had a baby dropped on his doorstep, and she was supposed to be helping solve his problems, not giving him existential issues to grapple with.

The fire flickered to life, and she closed the door.

"I'm sorry," she said. "I didn't mean to unload that onto you."

"It's fine." His voice was calm and quiet. "So you don't feel safe. Is that what you're saying? In the Amish life, I mean. You don't feel like you're really protected."

Grace let out a slow breath. "*Yah*. That sums it up."

"And you feel safe…with *Englishers*?" he asked.

She sucked in a slow breath. "I feel safer. *Yah*. I have medical insurance through work. I can go to the doctor whenever I want. I don't need to get permission or explain myself to my community."

Taylor had fallen asleep, and Ben looked down at her. He chewed on the inside of his cheek, his expression veiled. Then he looked up.

"As a man, that's tough to hear," he said quietly. "That a woman in one of our communities wouldn't feel protected and safe. That's our job—us men. We have one job, really. We're here to provide and take care of you. Maybe a community can't protect quite as well as a husband can."

"Or a father?" she asked, then shook her head. "You see, that doesn't make me feel safe anymore, either. I can't count on someone else for that. I need to be allowed to do what I need to do! A woman needs to be able to see to her own health. And she needs to be taught what tests she needs done regularly to make sure she lives past the age of twenty-two."

Her words stuck in her throat, and she blinked back some unexpected tears. That was how old Tabitha had been when she died. Twenty-two, with all of her life ahead of her, and so much love still saved up for the family she wanted.

"Your sister?" he guessed.

"*Yah*, my sister," she said. "She didn't know that she should have had medical checkups. She thought that my parents knew best, and that the bishop did, too. And she died. So I feel safer when I've got the freedom to go see a doctor, to get blood tests, to talk to a doctor when I'm not sure about something. *That* makes me feel safer."

Ben was silent for a moment, and then he went over to the cradle and laid Taylor down.

She squirmed, but he kept a hand on her until she settled again, and then he met Grace's gaze and licked his lips.

"I, for one, do believe in the *Ordnung*, and in my *Gott*-given duty to protect the women under my care," he said quietly. "And that doesn't mean holding them back. It means championing them when they need it."

He looked so earnest, so honest, so noble.

"I think you're a good man, Ben," she said.

"And I told you before, but I meant it. I consider you to be my responsibility while you're under this roof. I hate the thought of you not feeling safe. While you're here, with me, you are." He paused. "For what that's worth."

"I know," she said. "Don't worry."

She felt safe enough for a few days here, but would she feel safe coming back to an Amish community again and living under the *Ordnung*? Would she trust her life to an Amish community? But telling him that wouldn't help anything. When she left this house with the baby, this family could go on with their Amish life, and her heresies would melt into the background.

"Where's the coffee?" she asked, changing the subject. "I think you'll like my homemade lattes. They're good."

Grace would make those lattes and let Ben

tease her about Coffee Soup. And when the snow stopped, she'd go back home and find her balance again.

The problem with being born Amish was that there was always a part of her heart that tried to come back, and that fragile, hopeful part of her was always disappointed when it wasn't possible. She loved her Amish upbringing. *That* was the problem.

As well-intentioned as it all was, she just couldn't trust the life she was born into to protect her.

Ben took a mug of hot tea up to his sister's bedroom, but she was sound asleep, so he left it on the bedside table. In a matter of weeks, Iris would be married. He was happy for her, and he liked Caleb a lot, but there was still a small space in his heart that felt a swell of melancholy. Things were changing.

Iris was the sister closest in age to himself. She was three years younger, and in school, he used to tease her mercilessly until one day another boy decided to do the same, and Ben had gotten into a fight with him. Ben could tease his sister, but no one else could. That day, he'd grown up a little bit, and he'd stopped teasing her quite so much.

It wouldn't be Ben's job to stick up for her

anymore… But he did wonder if he'd done well enough by her.

Iris stirred and opened her eyes.

"Hi," Ben said.

"Ben?" She pushed herself up onto one elbow. "Is something wrong?"

"No," he said. "I just brought you some tea. I thought it might help."

"Thank you." She reached for the cup and took a sip. "I can get up and start cooking—"

"No, you rest," Ben said. "We've got it under control. We'll have leftovers for lunch, and I can bring some up to you."

"How come you're being so nice?" Iris asked, lying back down on her pillow.

"I'm always nice," Ben said with a laugh.

His sister gave him a rueful smile. "Relatively."

"Look, Iris," he said, sobering. "If Caleb isn't taking care of you properly, I want you to tell me."

She blinked at him and gave him a funny look. "I'll be fine, Ben."

"I'm serious," he said. "I'm still your brother, okay? Married or not. And I'll still have your back."

Iris eyed him uncertainly. "What's going on?"

"I was just thinking," he said.

"He loves me, Ben," Iris said. "You don't have to worry about Caleb."

"I know. Go back to sleep," he said, suddenly feeling uncomfortable having said so much. "Just thought it needed saying."

He gave his sister a nod and then left the room, closing the door behind him. Grace didn't feel safe in an Amish community, and that stuck like a barb in his chest. Did the women in his community worry about the same things that Grace did? Was this a more widespread problem? Maybe the men had some discussing to do about their responsibilities toward the women they protected.

Or maybe Grace had a point that it came down to letting a woman take care of her individual health needs herself and making sure she had access to enough money to make it possible.

Ben headed back downstairs. As he emerged into the kitchen, he paused at the cradle to look at the sleeping baby. It was a big responsibility to be an Amish man. Women and girls weren't there to just take care of the women's work. They were the heart of the home—the reason a man came back every day. *Gott* had placed their happiness and safety into the men's hands. And

Ben was confident that one day *Gott* would hold them accountable for the families He'd blessed them with.

Grace put a mug on the table, a white froth wobbling on the top, and it tugged him out of his thoughts.

"It's ready," she said with a smile. "This is a latte. Well, my approximation, at least."

"Yah?" He came to the table and picked up the mug, taking a small sip. It was sweet and delicious. He shot her a smile. "It's good."

"If you put some chocolate in that, it's a mocha," she said. "And there are all sorts of different flavors they add, like maple or pumpkin spice."

"Pumpkin?" He grimaced. "That belongs on a plate, not in a cup. Is that like their green smoothies? I saw those in Pittsburgh. They're even bringing them to the English side of Redemption. They seem to use kale and spinach and whatnot. All sorts of things that don't belong in a cup."

"It's not actually pumpkin. It's cinnamon and nutmeg and some allspice…some cloves. They just call it that—reminiscent of pumpkin pie. It's a fall thing."

He pondered that a moment and took another sip. *Englishers* had their ways.

"Well, I like this," he said. "I mean, I stand

by strong, black coffee, but this is like dessert in a cup. I still want to dip a crust of bread in this."

Grace chuckled. "I wouldn't stop you."

Ben rose, took a piece of bread from the bread box and dipped it into the frothy coffee. Call it what they wanted, this was Coffee Soup—albeit a really good version.

Hannes coughed in the other room, and then Ben heard him grunt as he got up.

"How are you feeling, *Daet*?" Ben asked as the older man came into the kitchen.

"A little better," Hannes said. "Is that Coffee Soup?"

Ben looked over at Grace, waiting to see what she'd say. He met her gaze, suppressing a smile. Grace shook her head and then shrugged.

"Yah," she said. "It's Coffee Soup. Do you want some?"

Ben chuckled at that. She'd relented, it seemed.

"Please," Hannes said, giving Ben a curious look. "That would be great. My *mamm* used to make that for me. We *kinner* would all sit around the table and use up the last scraps of dry bread, and it was the biggest treat."

Grace went about getting a latte for Hannes,

and Ben went to fetch his *daet* a piece of bread to go with it.

"The *Englishers* call this a latte, *Daet*," Ben said. "They don't dip bread in it."

"Then they're missing out," Hannes said, and he dunked his bread into the mug.

They were Amish. Other people might have discovered the combination of strong coffee and milk as well, but the Amish had their ways, too. There was comfort in that.

Ben looked toward the window and watched as the snow swirled past the glass. He'd have to dig a path to the chicken house and another one to the barn just to keep it passable, because that snow kept coming down.

Like any Amish man, he worked as hard as he did to take care of the people he cared about, and his family needed him right now. As did Grace and the baby she'd come to collect. His gaze kept moving back to her, with her hair in a ponytail and her hands on her hips as she watched Hannes dip his bread into his mug. She was quickly becoming a part of things here—for him at least. She was warming a spot in this home that he hadn't noticed before...

He pushed the thought from his mind. He liked her. He was attracted to her, even, but that didn't mean anything. She was right. As interesting as he found her, she was the social worker.

This might be easier if he found her a little less pretty.

That evening, his chores were done. The path from the house to the stable, and at least a good start of a path that led toward the barn, had been shoveled. Ben came inside, his muscles aching and tired. Grace was the only one in the kitchen, and she stood at the sink, washing dishes.

"Hi," he said as he hung his coat up on the hook and came into the warmth.

She put a finger to her lips. "Taylor just fell asleep."

"Are my *daet* and sister in bed?" he asked softly.

Grace nodded. "I made some soup for them. Their fevers seem to have broken, but they still need rest."

"That's good news," he replied, and he picked up a towel to help her dry.

Grace moved over to make space for him next to her, and he picked up a dish to dry. She was so close to him, and he could make out the soft scent of cooking that still clung to her. She'd taken her hair down, and it hung loose behind her shoulders, shining softly in the low light. He sucked in a breath, steeling himself.

"There's more soup on the stove," she said.

"I'm okay," he said, and he picked up a dish to dry. He was hungry, but he wanted to help her with the dishes first. Her arm brushed against his as she worked, and all of his attention suddenly focused on that one spot on his arm. Outside, he could blame the weather, and his protective instinct could be explained away. What about in the warm, dry house?

"I kind of like this. I miss having people to take care of," she said quietly.

"Yah?" At least being stuck here with them wasn't a punishment.

She looked up at him, her gaze quick, shy. "If it weren't for this storm, I'd be at home right now with the TV on for company."

"Why didn't you ever move back with your parents?" he asked. "You missed them—I know that. You miss this—" he glanced around the kitchen "—an Amish home. Are you not welcome there?"

"I am welcome," she said. "And I visit them from time to time, so it's not like I'm cut off from my family completely. I never was baptized, so I wasn't shunned. But there are so many difficult conversations, and my parents

see things the way they see them. They're..."
She sighed. "They're Amish to the core."

"So am I," he said.

"But I don't owe you anything," she said.
"And I do owe them."

He smiled at that. Yes, children did owe
their parents something after having been
raised and loved, provided for.

"What are they like?" he asked, picking up
another dish to dry.

"My *daet* is a deacon," she said. "So there
is a lot of pressure there to do things well, and
for his *kinner* to follow in suit."

"Ah..." That did sound like a high-pres-
sure situation.

"And my *mamm* is fun-loving, kind, and a
great cook," Grace said. "She prays... I mean,
she really prays. I used to wake up early in
the morning, and I'd find my *mamm* already
on her knees in the sitting room, praying. I
asked her why she would give up her last hour
of sleep in the morning, and she said it was
the only time that no one would ask her for
anything and interrupt."

"Did she get results?" he asked.

"Yah." She nodded. "She'd pray and *Gott*
would move..." Tears welled in her eyes,
and she blinked them back. "With my sis-

ter, my *mamm* prayed and prayed, and nothing happened."

Maybe it had simply been *Gott*'s will, but Ben wouldn't say that. The Amish beliefs didn't seem to comfort her.

"Were you angry?" he asked instead.

"Yah." She nodded, turning toward him. Her clear gaze met his. "I was. Because for all of my mother's praying, action is still necessary. And when I told my *mamm* that I thought we needed to be more careful with our checkups and our health in our community, she refused to listen to me. No *action*. She said the bishop and the elders needed to talk about it. It needed to be debated and brought before the counsel. But what about us women?"

"Maybe she blamed herself for not catching your sister's illness in time," he said. "Maybe she couldn't face that thought."

"Maybe." Grace swallowed. "There is a time when prayer like that is pure faith. I know it. And for a lot of my mother's life, it was faith. And then there comes a time for action, and staying on her knees was just paralyzing her."

But he couldn't see how prayer could be anything but good.

"I'm sure she's praying for you, too," he said.

A rueful smile touched her lips, and she turned back to washing the dishes.

"I want my mother's prayers," she said. "But do you know what I need more immediately? For her to talk to me and listen to what I'm feeling. The last time I visited, she closed off, wouldn't listen. She was right and I was wrong—at least in her mind. And after spending all day ignoring my arguments and worries, she then prayed all night. She could have talked to *me*. I was furious."

Grace rinsed the last dish and pulled the plug just as the baby started to cry. It was a low, sad cry, and it stabbed right down to Ben's heart. Grace crossed the kitchen to the cradle. She bent and tenderly scooped the baby up. She checked her diaper. Then she propped the infant up on her shoulder and rubbed her back.

"There, there…" she murmured, and she swung back and forth.

Ben watched her for a moment, the baby's cries going on without pause.

"I don't mean to talk about these things with you," she said. "You don't need to hear about my loss of faith."

Neither had her own parents, apparently. That seemed unduly harsh. Or maybe they just didn't know how to discuss those things, because Ben didn't know how to, either.

"Maybe I want to hear about it," he said. "It might help me to understand what went wrong for you."

Even though it made him uncomfortable, he wanted to hear what went on in her thoughts.

"You'd be the first to really want to hear it," she said. The baby continued to cry, and she shifted her attention to the infant. "You poor thing. You want your mother."

Ben leaned back against the counter. Grace was silent for a moment and then began to sing softly, "You are my sunshine, my only sunshine…"

It was a sweet song, one he'd not heard before, but it didn't seem to help. She switched to a different song—another English lullaby. It was no use, either. Then Grace suddenly stilled, and her gaze met Ben's.

"I wonder…" He saw the words on her lips rather than heard them. And then she started to sing a different song—a familiar one Ben remembered from his own childhood.

"*Gott* made the sun and the moon and the stars up above," she sang softly. "He made your *mamm* and your *daet* and filled them with love. *Gott* made the goats that bleat and the cows that moo. And then, dear *bobbily*, *Gott* made you."

And little Taylor calmed. Her crying stilled, and she hiccoughed a couple of times, her little blue gaze searching Grace's face intently.

"Your *mamm* is Amish," Grace whispered to the baby in Pennsylvania Dutch. "Isn't she?"

Grace's gaze snapped up to meet Ben's, and he felt the air rush out of his lungs. The note hadn't seemed Amish…and the baby had been dropped off in a car. But still…

It was possible.

Chapter Seven

Grace awoke early the next morning, before the sun was up. Her watch said it was just after four o'clock, and the baby was still sleeping, her little soother bobbing up and down as she sucked in her sleep. Grace pushed her covers back and got up as quietly as she could. Iris blinked her eyes open and pushed herself up onto her elbow. She reached for a water glass.

"How are you feeling?" Grace asked softly.

"Getting better," Iris replied.

"I'm glad to hear it," Grace whispered. "I can take care of breakfast this morning—"

"No, no," Iris said. "I can do the cooking. I'm on the mend."

Grace stopped at the window and pulled back the curtain. The snow was still coming down, but not as heavily anymore. She could see to the fence posts that edged the field in the predawn gray, and the snow was so deep that only the tops of the posts were visible, capped with top hats of snow.

In the hallway, Grace could hear Ben's footsteps.

"I'll take care of the baby's diaper and get her fed," Iris said, pushing back her covers and sitting up. "*Daet* seemed pretty sick last night. If you would help Ben outside, it would be very kind."

"Of course," Grace said. "I agree. Your father needs to get better before he goes out into that weather again."

She pulled on the pants she'd worn underneath her dress the day before. Iris watched her, her expression unreadable.

"It's so cold out there," Grace said. "I'm not used to it."

"But you're waking up at chore time without needing to be woken," Iris said. "And you're cooking in an Amish kitchen and doing chores on an Amish farm…"

"I'm burning food in an Amish kitchen," Grace said with a low laugh.

"Oh, you'd be fine with practice," Iris said. "You fit in around here better than you think."

Did she? Her Amish childhood was coming back, and she knew the work. She pulled on the rest of her clothes and combed her hair, leaving it loose around her shoulders this morning. She accepted a fresh sweater from Iris with a smile of thanks.

There were times she'd wake up at four in the morning in her English life and just sit in her living room with nothing to do but read her Bible and think. It was a pleasure to have that time alone, but there were occasions when it grew heavy and lonely. *Gott* was there with her, but she wanted more than company. She wanted to be needed by someone. And there were no morning chores in an *Englisher* apartment to fill the time. It was strangely comforting to wake up at this hour and have work to do.

"I'll see you at breakfast, then," Grace said.

"*Yah.* Thanks!"

Grace made her way downstairs and got to the kitchen just as Ben was coming inside with an armload of wood for the stove. He dropped it into the wood box and shot her a smile.

"Good morning," he said. "You're ready?"

"*Yah.* Your sister says she can handle breakfast, so you won't be subjected to my cooking this time."

Ben chuckled but didn't disagree. "Let's go."

Grace pulled on Ben's old coat, and she accepted the gloves he handed her. Ben picked up a kerosene lantern that was already glowing cheerily, and they headed outside into the dark cold.

The snowfall wasn't so blinding as it was yesterday, and Grace could see several yards ahead as they tramped toward the barn. It was deep, though, coming up to Grace's knees, and snow fell into her boots as she trudged forward. She had to lift her knees high to get through it, and the effort was made worse by the restrictive dress on top of her pants.

"You okay?" Ben asked.

"*Yah*, I'm—" She grunted as she pulled her boot up and took another step. "I'm getting stuck here."

"Let me help you." Ben reached for her hand. "This is where I shoveled yesterday, although you can hardly tell now."

He pulled her hand, and she leaned into his strength as she took another couple of big steps and emerged into snow that was less dense and not quite so deep. She breathed a sigh of relief. His hand over hers felt more natural this morning, and before he released her, he squeezed her fingers. She felt a smile tickle at her lips.

"This is better," she agreed.

He paused and looked like he wanted to

say something, but then his gaze went over her shoulder and back toward the house. He raised his hand in a wave.

"My sister is at the window," he said.

Grace turned to see a light glowing in the kitchen and a form in the window.

"That's how rumors start," she said. "And it isn't my reputation on the line here."

Ben shot her a grin. "I'm the vulnerable one, am I?"

"You're the one in need of a good Amish wife," she said. "So...*yah*. You'd best mind how things look."

She was joking now, and Ben laughed.

"You're easier to be around than other Amish women," he said.

"Because I'm not Amish?" she asked.

"No," he said, eyeing her. "I think you are Amish deep down. You're a lot more Amish than you think, at least."

"So why am I easier?" she asked.

"I don't know," he said. "I'm still trying to figure that out."

But his eyes sparkled with humor, and he turned, leading the way toward the stable. Grace followed in his footsteps, or as close to them as she could get. His stride was much longer than hers.

Ben had to kick snow out of the way of

the stable door to get it open. She went inside ahead of him. He grabbed a shovel and cleared a space so that the door would open and shut with ease. Then he leaned the shovel against the wall and pulled the door shut after them.

Without the icy wind and with the heat of the horses' bodies, the stable was relatively warm, and the horses shuffled their feet in their stalls. One horse nuzzled Grace's hair. She turned to see that long face next to hers. It nudged at her coat pocket.

"He wants sugar cubes." Ben pulled out a plastic bag from his pocket and passed it over to her.

Grace took a couple of sugar cubes out and let the horse eat them off her palm with those searching, velvety lips.

"I enjoy having you around," Ben said.

"Do you really?" she asked.

"You make life here a little more interesting." He reached out and ran a hand down the horse's neck. "Besides, I like you."

He didn't look at her as he said the words, and she could almost believe that he'd meant them for the horse, until his gaze flickered toward her—direct, intense.

"I like you, too," she said.

He smiled but didn't say anything more.

She took a couple more sugar cubes out of the plastic bag and moved on to the next horse. "I'm wondering about Taylor's mother."

"You think she's Amish," he said.

"Yah." She watched as the horse's lips gathered the sugar from her palm.

"There were a few girls who left the community and went English," he said. "It happens. Our community wouldn't be the only one. But I can't think of any girls we knew very well who would come to us in particular to leave a baby."

He pulled open the stall door and led the horse out to the opposite side the stable.

"What happens when you find her?" Ben asked.

"I do my best to help her," she replied.

"And if you weren't there, and she were at the mercy of social services agents with no direct experience of an Amish life?"

"Then…" She sighed. "Then, it would be more difficult for those agents to understand her situation. But there are a fair number of Amish runaways and people who come out of the community that we help. She wouldn't be alone."

"If she's Amish," he concluded.

"Yes, if," she agreed. "But the way Taylor reacted to that lullaby…"

It was almost the way Ben had. He'd stilled, stared at her. A familiar lullaby brought up emotion for everyone.

Grace shook out the last of the sugar cubes into her hand and moved on to the final horse.

"Be careful with him," Ben said. "He's powerful in the field, but he's not as tame as I'd like."

Grace paused and eyed the horse. He reached out, stretching his neck toward the sugar, and she kept her palm as flat as she could, giving the animal no excuse for a nip. She understood this kind of horse.

"You like to make trouble," she said to the horse.

"He likes to steal *kapps*," Ben said. "He'll snatch them right off a woman's head and then refuse to release it."

Grace couldn't help but laugh. "So he's a tease, too, is he?"

"It would seem," Ben agreed.

The horse nudged for more sugar, and she showed him the empty bag.

"Sorry," she said.

He reached for her hair, caught some in his teeth and tugged.

"Hey!" she said. Ben strode up to her side and patted the horse's nose.

"Let go," he said firmly.

The horse released her. Ben tugged Grace out of reach of those big teeth, then stroked her hair down. It was a tender gesture, one that seemed more instinctive from him. It seemed to take him by surprise, too, because he slowed, his hands still in her hair, which ran through his fingers. Her breath caught.

She licked her lips, and a little color seemed to touch his face. Embarrassment?

"I'm not used to being around a woman with her hair down," he whispered.

"Oh…"

"It's pretty," he murmured. "So soft."

"It's normal with the English," she breathed.

"I know." He twined her hair around his finger and then released it with a rueful smile. "I still like it."

She felt her face heat. "Thank you."

"*You're* pretty," he amended.

He'd told her that before, and having him say it again made her heart tumble.

"I should stop saying what I'm thinking," he added.

"I don't mind," she said.

His gaze moved over her face, stopping at her lips. There was something in his eyes she'd never seen before, something intent, tender…purposeful. If this were any other situation, she might think this man was going to kiss her, but…

Grace felt another tug on her hair, and she reached back with a breathy laugh to catch the hair the horse was pulling.

The horse released her hair. Ben put a hand behind her back and nudged her farther away from the horse, his touch firm, protective.

"We should get this stable cleaned out," he said, clearing his throat.

"Yah." Her heart fluttered in her chest.

This time, it wasn't just her reacting. She'd seen the way he'd looked at her, and he was feeling it, too. Something had been hanging there between them, tugging them toward each other.

Maybe Grace should be a little more careful. She wasn't just a guest with an Amish background. These weren't family friends, and this was no vacation. She was here in a professional capacity to bring a baby girl back to the office.

Not to become emotionally entangled with this very available, very attractive man.

She had to remember that.

Ben exhaled a cautious breath, and he glanced over his shoulder at Grace. She was filling a tin feed pan with some grain, her hair swinging past her face so he couldn't see her expression. And she didn't look entirely Amish, either, even with the dress. Those old trousers and boots sticking out the bottom made her look like an Amish and English hybrid, a woman who didn't fully belong in either world. Or maybe, more accurately, she didn't fully belong *here*.

So what was he doing? He'd said too much. He always did. She was pretty... And she was oddly comforting in this time of change and upheaval in his family.

Weddings were joyous events, but they also brought a whole lot of adjustment. Families inevitably changed when people got married.

But it wasn't just that. He was forgetting himself. He'd been seriously thinking about kissing her.

And at the reminder, an image of her face, her lips slightly parted, her sparkling gaze meeting his so easily...

Had he offended her? He wasn't sure.

Stupid, he mentally chastised himself. Was he seriously going to cross that line with a social services agent?

Ben put his back into the work of mucking out the stalls. He needed to get his balance. There was something about this storm—the isolation of it, maybe—that was getting to him. Women like Grace weren't for him. She had a life of her own, and he needed a good Amish woman by his side. If he wanted to get married any time soon, he'd better keep his boots on the ground.

When they finished with the stables, he pushed open the door and led the way out into the biting wind. Smoke emerged from the house chimney, and the downstairs was aglow in lamplight.

"Let's feed the calves and then go back for breakfast," Ben said.

"Sure."

"Unless you wanted to head in now. I can do the calves on my own," he said.

"No, let's do it," she said. "An extra person makes it go faster, doesn't it? Besides, if I go in, I suspect your father will come out to help you. Let's not give him the excuse."

Ben shut the door behind them.

"That's a good point," he said. "You sure you don't mind?"

"It's nice to get back onto a farm for a little while," she said. "It's good for the soul."

Having her here with him seemed to be good for his soul, too. He felt a little more hopeful and a little more energetic. As they plunged into the snow again, he reached back and caught her gloved hand in his. Holding her hand felt natural this morning, and he helped support her weight as she struggled through the deep snow after him.

"Is it just me," she panted beside him, "or is the snow slowing down?"

Ben looked up at the gray sky, softening pink in the east as the sun came up. The snow wasn't coming down so hard anymore, and the sky had a different look to it.

"Yah," he said. "The clouds seem higher, too. It might be letting up."

For the farm, that was good news. For his sister's wedding plans, too. But for him, personally, he could use another day of heavy snowfall, just for an excuse to keep on enjoying Grace's company. There was something about a dense veil of snow that made things feel possible that otherwise weren't.

"Are you anxious to get back to Vaughnville?" he asked, shortening his stride again to accommodate her. She was breathing hard, and they slowed to a stop while she caught her breath.

"Well, I'm going to have a lot of work to catch up on," she huffed. "And there's a baby to account for. It's…a big deal."

"I could see that," he admitted with a rueful smile. "But a winter blizzard is bigger than all of us."

"It is," she agreed, and they started forward again. "My *mamm* used to say that *Gott* used the winds and the waves to get people's attention for as long as we have recorded history. I used to wonder what *Gott* was trying to say to me during storms when I was a little girl."

It was an interesting thought—one that hadn't occurred to him before. He was normally asking *Gott* to get them through a storm, not wondering if *Gott* was using it for anything bigger. But for this one—he looked around, at the blowing snow, the drifts, the gold-tinged light of a sunrise veiled by clouds… Was *Gott* at work in this one, Ben wondered?

"But it's different being a girl inside the house," Grace went on, her fingers tightening in his grasp. "I was always looking out the window, wondering if *Daet* was okay and how long he'd be. I think I like this better."

"Being out in the storm?" he asked.

"*Yah.* At least I know what's happening," she said. Her gaze flickered up toward him. "Part of my problem is that I'm not patient. I hate just sitting around waiting for results or for a man to do something. I'd rather roll my sleeves up, so to speak, and just get it done, even if it's men's work." She paused. "That's not very feminine, is it?"

Ben shrugged. "It's honest. And it's effective, too. You forget—I'm a big fan of people just saying what they think, instead of saying what they're supposed to."

She laughed as they pushed forward through the deep snow.

"We're supposed to trust," she said, "have faith. And I'm out there in the world trying to fix it. I'm taking on a storm, as it were."

Ben was silent for a moment, processing her words. She'd left the Amish life, but she was certainly following the Christian path of helping others. He couldn't argue that.

"I think you make a difference in a lot of lives," he said at last. "And that's more than a lot of us do. You answer to *Gott*, not us."

"You are not a typical Amish man, Ben," she said.

"That's generally my problem."

Another gust of wind brought swirling flakes with it. The snow might be letting up a little, but it hadn't stopped yet.

Inside the barn, they set to work milking the cows and feeding the calves. Ben made sure to focus on his work a little more closely and didn't give himself the opportunity to get too close to Grace again. He needed to be careful. There was something about her that just tugged him in, and he couldn't let himself feel more than he should. If he couldn't hide his feelings very well, it would be embarrassing later.

When the work was done, they plunged back out in the snow. Ben carried a covered tin bucket with frothy milk, being careful not to let it spill as they followed their original footprints as far as they could until they veered off toward the house. Wood smoke scented the air, and Ben's stomach rumbled.

As they got to a particularly deep drift just before the house, Ben paused and looked toward the white hump that was her car. Snow covered over all sorts of things, including the very large reminder that Grace wasn't Amish anymore. He then glanced toward the house and the glowing windows. His sister passed in front of one of them.

He hadn't held Grace's hand this time, but the snow was deep, and she'd struggle without his help.

"Grab onto the back of my coat," he said, lifting the bucket of milk a little bit higher. He felt her take hold of his coat, and he plowed through the snow ahead of her, carrying both of them through the deep snow. When they got through the drift, breathing hard, he looked back at her. Her cheeks were pink from the cold and exertion, and her eyes shone in the light from the windows. She was so beautiful that it nearly stole his breath.

"Um—" He cleared his throat. "Could you get the door?"

Grace smiled and brushed past him, going up the steps first. What he was feeling for her wasn't safe, because when she left, he was going to miss her.

Ben looked up at the house, at the thick cover of snow on the roof, curving forward and hanging down from the eaves like frozen waves. That snow that hung in such stunning formations, blown by days of wind and driven snow, grew like it was almost alive. It was heavy, moist and wet under a sheet of ice, pressing into the roof.

He'd have to get up there and shovel it off as soon as this storm was over, or they'd end up with leaks in their ceiling.

Beautiful things could take a man's breath away and still be dangerous to everything that protected them. They could erode their safety and security. They could cause damage.

"Are you coming?" Grace called. She held open the screen with her body, and the door was open a few inches.

"Yah!"

Ben followed her up the steps and into the mudroom, and put the heavy bucket of milk down on the bench. Then he shut the door solidly behind them. It was a storm—that was all. And soon enough they'd all be back to their regular rhythms, their previous plans.

The house smelled of pancakes and hot coffee, and when he glanced into the kitchen, he saw his *daet* sitting by the stove, the baby in his arms.

"How are you feeling, *Daet*?" Ben called.

"After sleeping in like an *Englisher*, I feel a lot better." Then his cheeks blazed. "I didn't mean that as an insult. No offense intended, Grace."

"None taken," she replied, poking her head around the corner. She hopped on one foot as she stepped out of her boots.

"She's tougher than your average *Englisher*, anyway," Ben said, pulling off his coat. "How about you, Iris? How are you feeling?"

"I feel well enough to cook," she replied.

They were all on the mend. Everything would be fine…

"Is it just me, or…" Iris's voice faded away, and she shaded her eyes, looking out the window.

Ben looked down at Grace, and she had a

dusting of fine snow on her hair. He brushed it, the sparkle of crystals already melting into tiny droplets of water on her hair. He shouldn't be acting so familiar with her, and if he was a different man, he'd claim that he was feeling brotherly. But he was an honest man to a fault, and he wasn't feeling anything like a brother. He liked her...more than liked her. He felt protective of her, and he was starting to feel a rare, tender friendship emerging between them. He had a feeling this was the very thing he'd been waiting for...embodied in the wrong woman.

Ben was a glutton for punishment, wasn't he? They exchanged a small smile, and Ben passed Grace and headed out of the mudroom and into the kitchen.

"Is it just you, or what?" Ben asked his sister.

Iris was standing by the window, her attention fixed outside.

"Has it stopped snowing?" she asked.

Ben crossed the kitchen and looked outside. She was right. The snow had stopped, and the white mantle glistened in the faint light of early morning, broken only by their footprints leading out toward the stable and the barn.

"Yah," he agreed, and felt a sinking feeling inside of him that he couldn't quite explain. "It looks like it has."

Chapter Eight

Taylor squirmed in Hannes's arms, and Ben watched as his father rose to his feet.

"Son, would you mind being on baby duty for a bit?" Hannes asked.

"Sure, *Daet*." Ben came over and accepted the baby from his father's arms. She squirmed again while Ben got her settled up on his shoulder, and she nestled closer to his neck. Hannes accepted a mug of coffee from Iris and sank into a kitchen chair.

"Grace thinks that Taylor's mother might be Amish," Ben said, sitting down next to his father. He patted Taylor's back gently, and the baby's tiny fingers gripped his shirt. He smoothed a hand over her downy head—so fragile, so much in need of love.

"*Yah?*" Hannes frowned. "But the mother

arrived in a car. The baby's name...the note...
None of that seemed Amish."

"I know," Ben agreed. "But when the baby
wouldn't sleep last night, Grace and I tried
everything to calm her, and the only thing
that did was an Amish lullaby."

Hannes frowned. "Maybe it's just an effective tune."

"It felt like more than that," Ben said, shaking his head. "It's hard to explain."

"An Amish girl who went English, maybe?"
Hannes guessed.

"That's what I'm thinking," Ben replied.
"Are there any girls who jumped the fence in
the last year or more that we know?"

Hannes shook his head slowly. "There are
a couple...but none who had babies that I
know of. Unless it was kept secret. And why
wouldn't she bring the baby to her own family?"

"Or it could be a girl from a neighboring
community," Ben said. "I'd guess that the father of this baby is an *Englisher*, giving her a
name like Taylor."

Hannes nodded, and they both regarded
the infant for a moment. Who did this baby
belong to?

"I didn't realize she was an Amish baby,"

Hannes said quietly. "I might have felt a greater obligation to take care of the little thing for longer, give the *mamm* or her family a chance to come back for her."

"*Daet*, Iris is getting married," Ben said. "She's got a wedding to prepare for, and once she's married, she'll be starting a family of her own. While I suppose she could take care of the baby, it would be a lot to ask of a new bride. And I'm leaving for Shipshewana. How are you expecting to care for a baby?"

Hannes sighed. "I'm not. Maybe I could have handed her over to the bishop and his wife."

"You didn't suspect she was Amish," Ben said. "And in that letter, the mother didn't even give a hint of it. You did the right thing with the information you had. You can't save the whole world, *Daet*."

"Advice you should take to heart, yourself, son," *Daet* said with a meaningful nod.

Yah, it was advice that his father had given him a few years ago with Charity. Ben had acted like a big shot and taken her to the city. Those consequences were long-reaching. With Grace, he found himself wondering if he could offer her some sort of healing here…and it was silly of him, because she'd already made her choice for an English life, much like Charity. And here was this baby girl with an English name and what seemed like an Amish mother, and they couldn't be the answer for this child, either. Ben couldn't save everyone.

"*Yah*, maybe," he agreed.

Gott was the only one big enough to fill hearts. A man might want to be a hero, but life had a way of reminding him just how much power he really had. And it was never very much.

"The whole situation with this baby girl is just heartbreaking," Hannes said.

"*Yah*, it is sad," Ben agreed, and he looked up as Grace brought a platter of pancakes to the table. "But this little girl is in good hands, *Daet*. Grace knows our ways better than anyone else would in that social services office, and I think of anyone, she'd be sympathetic to a young, Amish single mother."

Perhaps *Gott* had brought Grace here during a storm so that she could sleuth out the truth. Maybe *Gott* was working in a baby girl's life right now, giving the people around her the information they needed to provide for her. And maybe *Gott* had brought Grace specifically because she was the one social services agent who would truly understand the subtleties of this case. *Gott* was a good and loving Father—even when He brought storms.

The women came to the table, and they all ate a hearty breakfast, even Hannes and Iris, whose appetites were now returning—an excellent sign. Taylor had a bottle, and Grace changed her diaper so that she could doze again, all warm and dry in Grace's arms.

"I need to shovel off the roof, *Daet*," Ben said.

"It's probably heavy, isn't it?" Hannes said.

"And icy," Ben replied.

"Hmm."

Ben didn't need to explain further. His *daet* understood the situation.

"I'll go get dressed, then," Hannes said. "We'll do it together."

"*Daet*, I'm sure I can handle it alone," Ben replied.

"You probably could. But I'm getting bored now, and it's a good sign that I'm feeling better. I'll help you."

Fifteen minutes later, both Ben and Hannes were outside. Ben leaned a ladder against the roof, and he gave it a shake to see if it was safe. With a shovel tucked under one arm, he climbed up the rungs until he was level with the roof and began to push the snow off. When he'd cleared off a big enough space, he climbed all the way up and continued the work.

When there was enough space for both of them, Hannes joined Ben on the roof. They continued to shovel the heavy snow over the edge and onto the ground.

The day was already warming up, and the snow got heavier. Ben grimaced as he tossed another shovelful of snow off the roof. It landed with a soft *thud* below.

"Do you mind if I ask you something?" Hannes said.

"Sure." Ben hoisted another shovelful of snow toward the ground.

"What's happening with you and Grace?"

Ben stopped working and turned to look at his father. "What do you mean?"

"I mean...what's happening there?" Hannes asked. "I know you well enough, son. I've seen you with a couple of girls who would have been happy to marry you, even with the unfortunate history with Charity. And this is different."

"Grace isn't looking for an Amish husband, *Daet*," Ben said. "She's taking Taylor, and she's going home to Vaughnville. That's the plan."

Hannes turned back to shoveling, and Ben did the same, but for a moment, as their shovels scraped over shingles, Ben rolled his father's words over in his mind.

"How is she different?" Ben asked, turning back to his father.

"It isn't that she's different—although, obviously, she's not Amish anymore—but you're different," Hannes said. "You're… softer with her."

"Softer?" Ben pushed his hat back on his head.

"I saw you holding her hand," Hannes said.

Ben swallowed. "That was to help her get through the snow, *Daet*."

"To start with, maybe," Hannes said. "But she's a beautiful woman, and you're a man, aren't you? You've noticed."

"*Yah*, I've noticed," Ben said with a sigh. "I won't lie about that. But I'm not developing a crush or anything. I'm just…enjoying her company, I suppose."

"There's a very genuine attraction between the two of you, and that can be dangerous when you are worlds apart," Hannes replied.

"Between us?" Ben asked. Did this go both ways?

His father just raised his eyebrows as if the point was made. Ben rolled his eyes and turned back to the shoveling, being careful where he stepped so as not to slip. That was a steep fall to the ground.

"I'm not going English again, *Daet*," Ben said. "I can promise you that."

"I hope not," Hannes said. "Falling for a woman is a powerful experience, but a lifetime is long. If you marry a sweet Amish girl who wants a houseful of *kinner*, you will grow old surrounded by your children and grandchildren, and you'll have all the riches of a life well-lived. But if you marry a girl and go English—" Hannes shrugged "—you'll have an English life. And if you want the girl, but not the world she lives in, you'll never truly be happy."

"I've experienced the *Englisher* world during my *Rumspringa*, and I came home," Ben said. "Trust me, I understand consequences."

The Amish life protected them from so many pitfalls that the rest of the country suffered from. The Amish stayed close as a community, and they genuinely needed each other's support. They raised their children to love *Gott* and live humble, honest lives. They kept their families close, and they kept those connections over the generations. There was protection in their Plain ways.

Yet, even as he thought about the security of staying with his community, he was reminded of the woman inside who didn't trust those boundaries to protect her. She seemed to love the Amish life, but it hadn't been the "hedge of protection" it was designed to be. It had failed her sister.

Not everyone saw the fence as a blessing. And maybe the fence wasn't the blessing it was supposed to be for everyone.

So why, as Ben shoveled, was he thinking about ways to convince her otherwise, to show her that she was safe with an Amish community? That she was safe…with him?

Inside the kitchen, Grace listened to the scrape of shovels across the roof. She could hear the heavy tread of feet as the men worked, and every little while a shower of show would come down in front of the window.

Grace stood at the sink next to Iris, drying the dishes the other woman washed. Taylor was in the cradle near the stove, her eyes open, but quiet and happy for the time being.

"I wonder how long it will be until the snowplows come and clear out these roads," Grace said.

Iris shrugged. "It'll be a while. But we'll clear out our own drives and shovel paths to the neighbors."

"To Caleb," Grace said with a smile.

Iris chuckled. "Yes, to Caleb. I've missed him. I normally see him every day."

"Is everything ready for the wedding?" Grace put a dry dish in the pile beside her.

"*Yah*, for the most part," she replied. "All the clothes for the *newehockers* are made, my dress is ready, and our wedding quilt has been completed for a few months now. I started on it right after he proposed."

All the wedding details… It made Grace's heart squeeze just a little bit.

"What will you do when you leave?" Iris asked after a beat of silence.

"I'll go back to the office," Grace replied. "There are reports to write about Taylor, and I'll have to do some filing and then bring her to a foster home. I'll need to check up on some other clients, too. And after that, I'll head back to my apartment and water my plants."

She smiled at the younger woman. There wasn't much else to do… Except, she had been thinking that she wanted to write her parents another letter. She missed them, and even though she knew that she'd get a letter back filled with pleas for her to return that would stab deeper than a knife, she longed to tell them about this strange trip to Amish country and to ask about her siblings, cousins and extended family.

"That's it?" Iris asked. "That's all you'll do? After being gone for days?"

Grace knew what Iris was thinking. The work piled up in an Amish home—cooking, cleaning, gardening, sewing... It never stopped, and the need was always there.

"I do have those clients to look in on," she said. "There are families that are struggling, and I've been helping to connect them with community supports."

Iris looked at her blankly.

"Um...for example, I'm working with some young people who are going back to school again after dropping out," Grace said. "And I'm working with several single mothers who need help getting affordable childcare while they work. And there are elderly people in the community who need meals and medication delivered to them."

Iris nodded. "So, instead of working in your home, you're taking care of other people's families."

"Exactly like that," Grace replied. "And if we weren't there to help them, I don't know what they'd do."

Iris was silent for a moment, and Grace picked up a handful of cutlery to dry.

"Can I ask you something?" Iris asked, putting another dish onto the rack.

"Sure," Grace replied.

"What's it like having a career?" Iris asked. "I mean, working outside the home every day like that?"

Grace dried the forks and knives one by one, dropping them into the slots in the drawer. How could she explain this to a woman who'd never experienced an *Englisher* life?

"It's...a relief," Grace admitted.

"How?"

"Well, I don't have to worry about money, for one," Grace said. "I make enough to keep myself and put some into savings. And I don't have to wait for someone else to buy things for me or give me money for it. If I need something, I get it."

Iris frowned. "Did your family not provide very well?"

"It isn't that," Grace replied. "My parents were very loving and my *daet* worked very hard. It's just—" Grace groped around for the words "—I suppose it's easier not to have to ask, you know?"

"Is asking so terrible?" Iris washed the last dish and pulled the plug in the sink. "I think that asking builds relationships. It also keeps me from overspending or being wasteful."

"Sometimes you're afraid to ask?" Grace paused in her drying. "Do you ever...maybe not ask for something you need so that you don't bother anyone?"

Because that could happen easily enough, which Grace knew from her sister's experience. She'd held back mentioning her symptoms because it had been private and a little embarrassing, and the cost of seeing a doctor made her not want to bother her parents with it.

"No!" Iris shook her head. "I don't think we're understanding each other. It's just that, when I get married, Caleb is going to take care of the money and he's going to be the one who works and provides for us. And I'll be the one who takes care of our home and our *kinner.* I think there are some things that men are just better at, and I like having a man who can take care of things."

Things men were just better at… Grace used to agree with that. But now, she was a woman with a career, and she was good at it. She was educated. She'd learned by experience that that wasn't true.

"And if you weren't getting married?" Grace asked. "If you were staying single?"

"Then my father would provide for me until I did," she said.

"And if your chances at marriage were getting thin?" Grace asked.

Iris's expression softened and she nodded.

"Well, then I'd need a job, I suppose," Iris replied. "I'm sorry, I didn't realize that you'd reached that point—"

"I'm not looking for pity," Grace said quickly. "And with the *Englishers*, I'm not exactly an old maid yet."

"Oh, that's good." Iris smiled hesitantly. "But don't you want a man to take over that part of things? I mean, as it is, you have to do it all. You have to work, take care of the money, take care of your home… I mean, wash day alone is so much work."

"We have laundry machines," Grace said. "I put the wash in, and a bell dings, and I move the clothes into the dryer, and then it buzzes and I fold it. I can do three loads an evening while I watch TV, if I need to, but it's only me. I might do two loads a week."

Iris was silent. "So you don't need a husband, then."

Grace dropped her gaze. "Of course I do. I don't need love and companionship any less just because I can take care of the chores all myself."

Iris wiped the counter, her expression clouded.

"Iris, the one thing that worries me—" Grace cleared her throat. "I don't want to overstep, but this is what happened to my sister. She had medical symptoms. And she didn't want to bother anyone or to waste the family money, so she didn't mention it. She ended up dying of uterine cancer—entirely preventable if she'd seen a doctor once a year like she should have been doing."

Iris looked up. "I don't have anything wrong with me."

"I'm not suggesting you do," Grace said. "But please, please, see a doctor yearly. I know it's an expense, but it could save your life. And if you notice any changes in your body, or things that worry you at all, see a doctor."

"Like you say, that's pricey, but I understand what you're saying."

"Your husband will need to take care of the money and the farm," Grace said. "But you have to take care of yourself, okay? There are some things a man can't be expected to do—like canning the food, or planning the meals, or…knowing what you need medically. That's too much to ask of him. But you need to take it seriously, because if anything happens to you as the wife and mother, everything falls apart."

Iris was silent, and Grace wondered if she'd said too much. It wasn't Grace's place to lecture a young woman on how to act in her marriage. She had family members and close friends who would give her advice.

"Caleb will take good care of me," Iris said. "I know the people you help don't have families, but I do. And Caleb loves me."

The younger woman was closing off. This wasn't a conversation she was comfortable with.

"*Yah*, I know," Grace said, forcing a smile. "I'm sure he's a good man, and you'll be very happy."

Grace had intruded on this family enough, and she knew that her *Englisher* life was completely at odds with the Amish one here. If anything, this visit was showing her that while she missed her Amish roots, her ideals had changed, and so had her worries.

She went to the side window and looked out. Her car was under a snowdrift, just a soft white lump. Now that the snow had stopped, she'd leave just as soon as the snowplows could come and clear the roads. And then she'd be on her way back to her responsibilities, to her clients, to that sterile office in the social services building in Vaughnville where Grace always seemed to work longer hours than anyone else.

Her supervisor called her passionate and

hardworking. Her colleagues called her dedicated. Her church friends called her inspirational. But if Grace had to be completely honest, she was lonely. There was a certain coziness that came with a close Amish community that couldn't be found anywhere else, no matter how well-meaning the *Englishers* might be, and Grace was caught between two worlds.

Iris reached for a baby bottle and the tin of formula.

"I'll feed Taylor," Iris said.

"Would you mind if I went to dig out my car?" Grace asked.

Iris chuckled. "My brother will do it for you."

"He's already dealing with the roof," Grace said. "Besides, it'll make me feel better to get working on it myself."

"Right." Iris nodded, and she smiled faintly. "Well, I can take care of things in here. Feel free to go shovel snow."

Grace headed up the stairs to get those pants on underneath her dress, and as she pulled them up, she wondered if maybe she was more like her sister than she cared to admit. Grace didn't want to be a bother to this family, either. She didn't want to cause work for Ben. She'd rather just take care of things herself. That independent spirit was alive and well in the Amish communities, too. It wasn't from weakness that women held back, it was from propriety.

Grace came back down the stairs to see Iris cuddling Taylor close, and the baby slurping down a bottle of milk. Grace cast the younger woman a smile, and then went to put on the borrowed coat—more appropriate to shoveling snow than her dress coat. She pulled up the hood over her hair and stepped outside.

She had just pulled the door shut behind her when a wallop of snow dropped on her head, and Grace let out a cry of surprise.

"Oh!" Ben said from above, and then he started to laugh. "Sorry about that."

Grace looked up, shielding her eyes, to see Ben peering over the edge of the roof, a teasing grin on his face. He pushed his hat back on his head.

"Was that on purpose?" She laughed.

"No, honest mistake," he replied. "But still funny. What are you doing out here?"

"I want to dig out my car."

Hannes appeared at Ben's side, and the older man smiled ruefully. "In a hurry to head back to the city, are you?"

"Well, I don't think I have much hope of

that until the roads are cleared, but it would be awfully nice to just see my car again."

"We can do that for you," Hannes said.

"You shouldn't even be shoveling the roof, Hannes," she retorted. "I'll be fine! If I can help muck out stalls, I can dig out a car." She glanced around. "Is there a shovel I could borrow?"

"Just inside the stable," Ben said.

"Right. Thanks." She headed in that direction, stepping through the deep snow, following their earlier footprints to make the trek easier. It was less work getting around without swirling snow and biting wind. She retrieved a shovel from a corner of the stable and went back outside. The clouds were high now, and the sun was like a faint silver dollar in the sky, trying to shine through. Hannes came down the ladder, followed by Ben. They conferred for a moment, and then Hannes headed toward the side door.

Ben came over, his own shovel in one gloved hand.

"I'll help you," he said.

"I'm fine, Ben," she said with a shake of her head. "I didn't mean to interrupt your work."

"It's no bother," Ben replied. "*Daet* could use a break anyway. And forgive me for being extra Amish, but while I can ask you to help me out with the men's work, I can't exactly leave you to do it alone."

Grace couldn't deny that there was a certain comfort in being cared for.

"You feel trapped here, don't you?" he asked, and they headed toward the wave of snow that covered her car.

"It's the weather," she said. "What can you do?"

Ben pushed his shovel into the drift and lifted the heavy snow, throwing it to the side. He was much stronger than she was, and when Grace started to dig next to him, she noted that he could lift twice as much snow in a shovelful than she could. He really would make this job go faster.

"Thank you, Ben."

"Hey," he said, stopping and fixing her with his dark gaze. "Out there with your *Englisher* life, I don't know who helps you. I don't know who takes it upon himself to make sure you're okay and to make sure you don't work too hard."

"No one, really," she admitted. "I take care of myself."

Ben didn't answer for a moment, but that direct, intense gaze never left her face.

"I don't like that," he said, his voice low. "I don't mind saying."

"It's life," she said with a short laugh. "It's how things are."

"Well, here on this farm, you're a woman. And we take care of our women here."

Grace felt a shiver go up her arms that had nothing to do with the cold, and she nodded. "It's nice."

And it was. It was tempting, and warming, and it made her wish she could lean back into his masculine reassurance. Who didn't want to trust someone strong, handsome and intriguing to take care of her? But she couldn't, even if they weren't living in different worlds. Because as well-meaning as this man might be, she knew where the ideals fell short.

And he didn't.

Chapter Nine

Ben gave Grace a small smile.

Did she understand him? Somehow, she'd walked away from the Amish life, not trusting it to protect her, and he couldn't believe that the *Englisher* ways were any better for a woman. He'd seen enough of their ways during his *Rumspringa*. They made their women do it all—and oftentimes, the women had no other choice. A woman shouldn't have to be that strong. She should be able to rely on someone to make things easier for her. Women had enough to do in the home without having to worry about paying for it.

But a man taking care of the money and being protective wasn't a welcome opinion. He'd learned that in Pittsburgh.

He turned back to the shoveling, digging out deep wedges of snow. He unzipped his coat at the neck, and together they worked on removing that drift of snow. When his shovel hit the rubber tire, he paused and straightened. Grace used her hands to clear some snow off the door. The windows were crusted over with ice, and after pushing off what she could, she leaned against the car, breathing hard.

"It's going to be more difficult to get out of here than I thought," she said with a low laugh.

"So you are in a hurry," he said.

She looked up at him, her cheeks pink from the cold and exertion. "I'm getting a bit too comfortable, Ben. I need to get home."

"There's nothing wrong with being comfortable," he said.

She didn't answer, and he sensed she was embarrassed.

"I'm serious," he said. "That's not a bad thing. Maybe you're seeing what you were missing."

"Oh, it's never quite so simple as that," she replied. "I know exactly what I'm missing, and there is no replacement for it out there with the *Englishers*."

"Like what?" he asked.

"Community," she replied. "A world that makes sense... I'm not saying that the *Eng-*

lishers don't have their own ways and logic, but I've never quite settled in with them. I can't quite figure them out. So it's never been about not appreciating what I had in my Amish life. It's about growing past it, I suppose."

He squinted at her. "That sounds…a little insulting."

"I'm sorry." She winced. "I didn't mean it like that. I don't mean that living here isn't a wonderful life, but there are times of growth, and during mine, I grew outside the fence. I don't think I'd fit back in."

"You might be surprised," he said.

"There are some things that are required to live contentedly Amish," she replied. "And the most important thing is belief in the rules. You have to believe that the Amish way is the best way to live, and that it's safest and closest to *Gott*'s will. And I—" She swallowed. "I don't have that anymore. I don't think the Amish way is the only way! I don't think it's the safest for everyone. I'll never be able to settle back into it again and feel the same way I used to feel. That's gone."

"Right." He cleared his throat.

"I envy you." Her voice caught, and he tried to read her features.

"Me?" he asked. "You mean a man's freedom, or—"

"I mean your faith," she said. "I think it's wonderful, and I hope it never wavers and you're able to find a good Amish woman and have a nice, big family."

It sounded like a dismissal, and he eyed her for a moment.

"Thank you?"

"I don't think any of this is coming out right," she said. "Ben, I'm here as a professional. I'm doing my job. And I'm sorry if I've been overstepping the lines and complicating things between us."

Ben chuckled softly. "*Yah*, you arrived here professionally, but you can't hide behind your job with me, Grace Schweitzer."

"I'm not hiding behind it," she said. "It's a fact."

"*Yah*, and so is the snow," he replied. "And the cattle. And the hat on my head. But this—" he waggled a finger between them "—isn't professional at all."

"I know." She sighed. "I'm trying to apologize for it."

Ben shook his head. "The *Englishers* really have changed you if you're apologizing for a real, honest, human connection."

"Is that what this is?" she asked, and he

saw some nervous hope in her expression. Was she feeling guilty about letting down her guard? Was being open and honest with a man such a crime?

"Yah," he said. "You like me, Grace. That's what happened here."

Grace rolled her eyes and picked up her shovel again. "I do like you. You're…" She didn't finish.

"I'm what?" he pressed.

"You're special," she said, but she wouldn't meet his gaze. "You're kind, and interesting and…" She cleared her throat. "And like you or not, I need to get my car dug out if I'm ever going to do my job and bring little Taylor back to the office."

She had a point, but she'd also admitted that she liked him—and that warmed him. Whatever was sparking between them was something he'd never experienced before, not quite like this, and he wasn't ready to just let it go.

He plunged the shovel into the snow and covered his smile as he got back to work. If she wanted to see her car today, then she'd see her car. That was one thing he could do for her.

When the car was free of snow, Grace got her keys from inside and started the engine.

After it had been encased in its own personal freezer, she wanted to make sure that it would start.

"There," Ben said. "I'd better get back to shoveling off the roof."

"I can help you with that," she said. "Two shovels are better than one."

She lifted hers with a smile, and Ben pressed his lips together as if considering.

"I want to say yes," he said, his voice low. "But that's because I like being around you just a little bit too much, Grace. It's probably better if I do it alone."

Grace nodded. She'd been feeling that same attraction, and he was right to put the brakes on. Still, she felt a little embarrassed, too, that she wasn't the one to do it first.

So Grace went inside with Iris just in time for Taylor's diaper to need changing. Grace hung the coat up on a peg and came into the kitchen.

"I can change her," Grace said, and she scooped up the baby and carried her into the other room, where the changing pad and diapers waited.

This was why she was here—and if Ben could remember that, then she'd better, too. She tried to make the baby smile by touching her nose and gasping in surprise. Taylor kicked her little legs and stared up at her in curiosity, but she couldn't quite coax a smile out of the baby yet.

"We'll find a very nice home for you, Taylor," Grace crooned. "There will be people to love you, and cuddle you, and play with you…"

Her voice caught and she stopped. It was so hard not to let her heart get entangled in her job, but this case seemed to be doing just that…with both the baby and this Amish family. Was there a young Amish mother out there regretting her decision?

And was it fair that the thought of a young Amish mother tugged at her heart in a more personal way?

Whatever home they brought Taylor to, it very likely wouldn't be Amish, and those memories of an Amish lullaby would fade. The thought of this child forgetting such an intimate detail from her biological mother made Grace's heart tug. Grace might not be practicing the Amish faith anymore, but her childhood would always be a part of her…including the little lullaby that her own mother used to sing to her.

Gott made the sun and the moon and the
stars up above.
He made your *mamm* and your *daet* and
filled them with love.
Gott made the goats that bleat and the
cows that moo.
And then, dear *bobbily*, *Gott* made you…

Grace blinked back a mist of tears. She
couldn't allow herself to do that—to care
more when it touched her own upbringing.
She had to be fair and make sure her empa-
thy flowed just as much for people she didn't
immediately identify with, too.

"Oh!" Iris exclaimed from the kitchen.

Grace did up the last of the baby's sleeper
snaps and then scooped her up in her arms.

"What's happening?" Grace asked, coming back into the room.

Iris stood at the kitchen window, a smile
on her face. She coughed into her elbow but
didn't turn. Grace went up to the window
and looked out, too, and she spotted a figure coming across the snow in snowshoes. It
was a man—his clothing dark, his face bare
of a beard, and he moved with strength and
stamina, stepping across the deep snow in
the field.

"Who is it?" Grace asked, although she could guess.

"Caleb's coming over," Iris said, and she turned toward Grace with a glittering smile.

"He didn't waste time, did he?" Grace chuckled.

"I knew he'd come when he was able," Iris replied. "See? I told you he's a good man. The only thing that can keep him away from me is a blizzard."

"That's very romantic, Iris," Grace said. "I'm impressed."

"Yah," Iris said, turning back to the kitchen. "He's not the type to put it all into words. He's quiet, and I think he's only told me he loves me about five or six times, but his actions speak louder."

"It's the actions that matter," Grace had to agree.

"I hope you find someone like him," Iris said.

Yes, so did Grace. It had been her dearest hope since she was a young teen. Women who did find men who loved them dearly should never take it for granted—that was her opinion, at least. Because finding an honest, reliable man who understood a woman and loved her didn't come along so easily for everyone.

Iris went back to the kitchen and pulled

out a Tupperware tub of muffins. She arranged some on a plate and then reached for the bread.

"He'll be hungry," Iris said. "And he loves the sandwiches I make him."

"He probably loves anything you make him," Grace said.

"*Yah*...he does." Iris laughed, and she seemed almost like a different young woman now—brighter, almost sparkling—with her fiancé on the way.

Grace went back to the window and looked out. Caleb was closer now, and Ben came out of the stable and waved in the other man's direction. The sight of Ben made her own heart stutter just a little. She had to get that under control!

This family was happy here. That much was clear. And her own family had been happy in Grace's childhood home, too. There had been both laughter and earnest times. Her parents' faith had been so strong that Grace had never imagined a world where her mother's prayers didn't move mountains.

Ben turned, his gaze sweeping toward the house, and when he saw her in the window, he stopped. He didn't turn, or smile, or make any move, just met her gaze with a look so intense that Grace felt heat rise up in her cheeks.

Her breath was stuck in her throat, and she was about to wave when Iris said, "Is Caleb at the fence yet?"

Grace startled and looked toward the other woman.

"*Yah*, he's at the fence," Grace said. "He'll be here in a minute."

"Oh, that's good," Iris said. "You'll like him. Everyone does."

Grace looked out the window again, and Ben was gone—back in the stables, presumably—and completely out of sight. She missed him. As ridiculous as that would sound to say out loud, her heart ached just a little to find Ben no longer there. There was something about the man that got beneath all of her professional guards and reserves.

"I'll take the baby upstairs," Grace said. "I'll let you have some privacy with your fiancé."

Iris didn't argue, and Grace headed for the stairs, gently tapping the infant's diapered rump as she made her way up to the second floor. She let out a slow, wavering breath once she reached the top of the stairs.

What was it about Ben that could stop her heart like that? It was only a look—but this was the second time now that his gaze through a window had left her breathless.

* * *

What is wrong with me, Lord? Ben silently prayed. *Why can't I fall for a woman who is appropriate?*

Ben had seen Grace in that window, and it had taken him by surprise. It wasn't that he'd forgotten she was in the house, but when he saw her standing there, her frank gaze locked on him, he'd felt his heart skip a beat. Literally. People talked about that like it was a metaphor or something, but his heart had actually palpitated in his chest.

That was the feeling he'd been waiting for with a woman—the absolute certainty that she was the most beautiful creature in his world. And now he was feeling exactly that with a woman who was going back to her English life.

It seemed almost cruel.

Ben finished in the stable and then headed up toward the barn. There was a lot of work to be done, and he wouldn't lean on Grace any more than absolutely necessary. She had her own job to do, and the more time he spent with her alone, the more he was enjoying her company and feeling things he had no right to feel.

Help me to stop this, he prayed. *Help me to release whatever these feelings are and go in the direction You want me to go. She's English now, and I know that she can't be Your will for me.*

He'd been praying for guidance, and this plan to visit another community had felt... blessed. He'd felt *Gott* in it. Was this his Paul experience, of having a spirit that wanted to do things *Gott*'s way and a worldly heart that kept yearning for something else?

Except, whatever he was feeling for Grace didn't make him feel guilty, either...just conflicted. He hadn't done anything wrong. Not yet.

As Ben approached the barn, he heard the jingle of bells, and he turned to see the Lapp family coming across the field that separated their farms in a sleigh pulled by two strong quarter horses. Eli and Irene were in the front, and their teenaged daughter Rose was behind, one hand on her *kapp* to keep it in place. Neighbors—there was no sight quite so welcome after a big storm. Ben stopped and waved, and Eli, Caleb's father, reined the horses in within a few yards of him.

"Caleb couldn't wait for the rest of us," Eli said with a laugh. "How did you all hold up during the storm? We got back from seeing

Irene's aunt just as it blew in. We left early, which ended up being a blessing."

"We're okay," Ben said, and he stepped through the deep snow to get closer to the sleigh. "I'm glad you got back in time and weren't caught on the roads. That was some storm! And you all? Any damage? I would have gone over and checked for you if we weren't snowed in."

"No damage, thank *Gott*," Eli replied. "If this is any indication of the winter to come, we're in for a cold one, eh?"

"*Yah*, for sure and certain," Ben agreed. "Oh, Iris and *Daet* came down with a bad cold. And just before the storm hit, we had a baby dropped on our doorstep. Have you all heard anything about a local Amish girl with a baby?"

"What?" Irene Lapp stared at him in shock. "On your doorstep? Whose baby is it?"

"That's what we're trying to find out," Ben said. "Well… I suppose the police will be trying to find out now. At first we thought it was an English baby, but now, we aren't so sure."

Ben told the story as succinctly as possible, including Grace's arrival and the storm.

"Anyway, Grace will be taking the baby back to Vaughnville just as soon as the plows come through," Ben concluded.

"Poor little thing," Irene said, shaking her head. "She just left her?"

"The baby is in the house?" Rose asked hopefully.

"Yah, yah," Ben said with a grin. "And she loves to be held, so I'm sure she'll enjoy some extra attention."

"Once I've got the horses taken care of, Caleb and I will come and help you finish the chores," Eli said. "Let's let your *daet* rest, if he's been that sick."

"Thank you," Ben said. "I appreciate it. And do me a favor and don't mention that to *Daet*. I'm afraid he'll take it as a challenge. He was up on the roof with me earlier, shoveling it off."

Eli gave him a thumbs-up and flicked the reins, and the sleigh started off toward the house. Rose turned around to wave at him again, a bright smile on her face, very likely because she had the opportunity to cuddle a baby for the afternoon.

Eli was true to his word, and about twenty minutes later he and Caleb came into the barn to help Ben finish up the work. With the three experienced men working together, the chores went quickly. The calves and goats were fed, the cow was milked, and within a couple of hours, Ben, Eli and Caleb were marching back toward the house together as the sun sank down below the horizon.

"The snow up on your barn roof looks real heavy," Caleb said, looking back over his shoulder.

"It slides off every year," Ben said. "I think it should be okay."

"Hmm." Eli nodded. "*Yah*, it should be."

But all the same, Ben regarded the barn with that deep, heavy snow capping the roof like a wave. It was hard to make out much detail in the lowering light, but the snow would slide off…wouldn't it? The barn roof was much steeper than the house's roof—and much higher, too. There were only so many things a man could deal with at once.

Smoke curled up from the chimney on the house, and Ben could smell the good cooking as they came close. A kerosene lamp had been lit already, and it glowed cheerily through a window. From inside, he heard a peal of laughter, and he couldn't help but smile in response to it.

"I think the women started dinner," Eli said with a grin. "We brought a ham over. Hope you don't mind."

"I don't mind at all," Ben replied with a chuckle. "Thank you. We'll all eat well tonight."

They kicked the snow off their boots and

headed into the house. The smell of ham and potatoes and other fixings filled the home, and as Ben scrubbed his hands at the sink in the mudroom, he felt that old comfortable glow of being at home.

When they entered the kitchen, Ben spotted Grace standing at the counter, putting dinner rolls into a bowl. She looked up, and her gaze met his. A smile turned up the corners of her lips, and his stomach hovered in response. Eli looked over at him, the moment not lost on the older man, apparently.

"She's not Amish," Eli said.

"No, she's not."

They exchanged a look and didn't say anything more. They didn't need to. Caleb hadn't noticed. His eyes were only for Iris. Rose was holding Taylor, talking to her softly.

"You're back!" Iris said. "Dinner's almost ready."

Caleb headed across the kitchen and leaned in to say something in Iris's ear. She pinked and shot her fiancé a smile. His sister would be well cared for. She and Caleb were going to live with Hannes for the first few months, at least, and Iris would have her father's protection, too. The Amish ways were logical and had worked for generations.

But when Ben's gaze slid over to Grace,

her hair hanging loose and glossy around her shoulders, he felt that disconnect between the world he'd trusted and believed in and a different point of view. Grace was so close to being Amish... Amish-raised, Pennsylvania-Dutch-speaking...but her hair was down. That seemed to be Grace in a nutshell—so close to one thing, and yet not quite.

"So what will happen with the baby?" Irene asked.

Everyone else turned to look at Grace, too, and she looked up uncomfortably.

"We'll find her a foster home," Grace said.

"Someone will adopt her?" Irene asked.

"That is the hope," Grace replied. "There are a lot of families looking to adopt babies, so we will try to find her a loving home."

"Will you find her an Amish home?" Irene pressed.

"Are you interested?" Grace asked.

Irene's gaze moved toward her husband, and for a moment there was silence between them as the question hung in the air.

"I'm a grandmother already," Irene said with a sigh. "It's a big responsibility to start at diapers again."

But she was a sweet baby, and everyone cared about what happened to her.

"What about Thomas and Patience Wiebe?"

Iris asked. "They've just adopted a little boy, but I know they want to continue to grow their family."

Grace looked up. "That's right. There was an adoption in this community not so long ago. An *Englisher* toddler, right?"

"Yes, Cruise was two when they got him. And they have two *kinner* now who were English-born," Iris added. "Rue and Cruise. I think a little Taylor would fit right in."

"If this baby is one of our own, she might be able to stay Amish yet," Irene said. "*Gott* always provides."

Ben listened in silence as they discussed possible families in the area that might want to adopt a child. But what about the mother? Would she come back? Would she want her baby back again? If the mother dropped her child off with an Amish home, it might have been so that she could come back eventually. She might have hoped for some mercy.

"*Gott* also provides wives, Ben," Caleb joked, and Ben pulled his attention back to their guests.

"What's that?" Ben said.

"We were saying that *Gott* has plans, and we're interested to see which girl catches your eye in Shipshewana," Caleb said.

"We have friends out there," Eli added.

"Make sure you meet the Mast family. They have some lovely daughters. Any one of them will do."

Ben chuckled, but when he looked over in Grace's direction, he felt the humor fall away. This didn't feel right to be joking about, somehow. Not now. Something had changed, something that neither he nor Grace would admit to, but it had. Would he find a wife? Maybe...but his heart wasn't in it like it had been just a few days ago.

And maybe Ben was mistaken, but he saw the tension in Grace's expression, too.

"I think we're ready," Irene said, carrying the carved ham to the table.

"Let's sit down," Hannes said, and they all took their places. After some shuffling and settling, they fell silent and bowed their heads.

Ben bowed his head for a silent prayer, but he peeked up at Grace sitting across from him. Her eyes shut, and her lips moving... That was no ordinary blessing of the food. There was an earnestness that spoke of deeper worries.

What was she praying for?

Chapter Ten

Grace lifted her head when Hannes cleared his throat, and she looked around the table.

During grace, she'd been praying for her family back in Creekside, praying for their safety and for some softening of their hearts toward her. She doubted she could ever go back and live Amish with them, but she did want to visit more often…maybe spend a week or two with them at a time?

She missed her mother desperately. It was strange how weddings and babies—even when they were other people's milestones—brought her thoughts home. She missed her mother's wisdom, her faith so strong and her prayers so sincere. And yet that faith and those prayers hadn't been able to accept a daughter who went English.

Was Grace punishing herself by thinking

of going home again? Were these last few days with the Hochstetler family just a reminder of what she'd never have again unless she bent to their will?

"Grace?"

She pulled herself out of her thoughts as Ben passed her the platter of sliced ham.

"Thank you," she said, serving herself and then passing it on to Iris, who sat next to her.

"Are you okay?" Ben asked.

She nodded. "Fine. It's been a long time since I've had a meal like this."

"You don't cook for yourself?" he asked.

She shrugged. "I do, but it's only me eating most evenings, and I never buy a ham or a beef roast. It's too much food for one."

"There's something about feeding a houseful," Ben said.

She smiled at that, but it touched at a certain sadness inside of her, too.

"I do sometimes help serve the free meals at a homeless shelter," she said. "That was the last time I had a turkey dinner—last Thanksgiving."

Ben met her gaze thoughtfully. "You are the most Christianly Amish rebel I've ever met."

Grace laughed at that and passed Ben the

bowl of mashed potatoes. "I'll take that as a compliment."

It would have been nice if her parents could have seen that side of her life—the one they could be proud of, even if she wasn't living Amish. But they couldn't see past the fence.

The two families turned their good-humored attention onto Caleb next, teasing him about how very soon he'd be a married man, and they worried about his ability to grow a beard. Rose said she worried that he'd just get fat because Iris was such a good cook and Caleb had absolutely no self-control at the table.

There was much laughter and teasing, and Grace sat quietly, absorbing it all. When everyone was finished eating, they all bowed for another silent prayer, and then Grace helped Iris clear the table. They piled up the dirty dishes in the sink and on the counter to wash later on, and then they pulled out some board games to choose from. Iris started a big pot of tea on the stove.

Taylor woke in her cradle. Grace picked her up and cuddled her close, then went to the counter to fix a bottle. From the table, there was great discussion on whether they would play a game of Dutch Blitz or Pictionary.

Rose left the table and came up to where

Grace stood shaking the bottle of formula. The girl touched the swirls of downy blond hair on the baby's head.

"She's so cute," Rose said.

"She really is," Grace agreed with a smile. "Do you want to feed her?"

"*Yah!* I'd love to." A smile lit up the girl's face.

"I'm sure you have a lot of practice feeding little ones," Grace said.

"My three older sisters all have *kinner*," Rose said. "So I've done lots of bottles and diapers. But I like it."

Grace eased the baby into Rose's arms, and the girl popped the bottle into Taylor's searching mouth. The baby clamped down on it with a slurp. Grace smiled at the girl and watched as she moved over to a chair next to her mother.

The room felt like it was getting stuffy and tight. Everyone had turned their joking onto Hannes now, but she'd missed what they were teasing him about. The older man laughed heartily, his eyes sparkling, and then he doubled over into a coughing fit.

Grace fetched a glass of water and brought it to the table, putting it in front of Hannes, who picked it up and gratefully took a drink.

"Thank you, Grace," he said, still coughing.

Grace eased past the table and into the mudroom. No one seemed to see her go, and she stepped into those borrowed winter boots and pulled down from a hook the now familiar coat she'd been using during her visit here. She slipped outside and closed the door softly behind her.

The brisk breeze was welcome, and when Grace exhaled a slow breath, it hung in the air in front of her. The air was cold against her legs, but she couldn't go back inside for the pants. It would only attract attention.

The windows on her car, now free of snow, were covered in frost, and for a moment, Grace just stood on the stoop, feeling the tension seep out of her. Behind her, she could hear the muffled sound of voices and laughter from indoors, and she made her way down the steps, away from the house. The snow crunched under her boots, and she looked up at the sky. The clouds were gone now, except for a few wisps, and the stars glittered. In town, the sky was never this brilliant. The artificial light of signs and headlights, streetlights and windows all competed for the more glorious view of stars and the milky, almost full moon.

There was probably a lesson in this—the importance of the eternal over convenience, perhaps? Her *mamm* would say that anything that competed with the glory of *Gott* was a poor replacement.

Grace heard the door, and she turned to see Ben come outside. He pulled his coat on as he tugged the door shut behind him, and he angled his steps in her direction. She'd come out here for some time alone, but she found herself happy to see him, all the same. Ben came to a stop beside her and did up his coat.

"You aren't okay," Ben said, his voice low.

"I am," she replied. "You know, for how much I miss big family events, I'm not used to it anymore."

"Is that all?" he asked.

She was quiet for a beat. *"Yah."*

"Are you anxious to leave?" he asked.

She shook her head. "Actually, I'm not. I'm missing my own family in Creekside, quite honestly. And I'm missing—" *what I would leave behind here.* But she couldn't say that. She forced what she hoped was a cheery smile. "Don't worry. Just as soon as those plows come through, you'll be rid of me."

"I don't want to be rid of you," he said, and he didn't return her smile. He wouldn't let her jokingly get off the hook, would he?

"This stay on your farm might have been

unexpected," she said earnestly, "but I have enjoyed it. Very much."

"Me, too," he replied, and his dark gaze met hers. "Very much."

She sucked in a breath. What did she hope to gain from talking with him out here?

"You can go in and enjoy the games," she said. "I'm fine. I don't mean to ruin your fun."

Ben shook his head. "Nah, it's okay. My fun isn't ruined. Trust me on that."

Grace looked over at him and found his gaze moving over her with a tenderness that made her breath catch. She licked her lips and lowered her eyes.

"I think I need to accept that I'll never have this," she said softly. "And I'm sad about that."

"You really think you won't be part of an Amish family again?" he asked.

"I'm part of my own family," she said. "I just don't think I'll ever find this easy, happy family relationship. It'll stay hard."

He leaned toward her, his sleeve pressing up against hers. "You aren't as scandalous as you think," he said.

"No?" *Convince my family of that.*

"Do you want to know why I have to leave Redemption?" he asked.

"To find a wife?" she said.

"*Yah*, but it's about more than finding girls

I'm not related to," he said. "I need a fresh start. I messed up."

"How?" she asked, turning toward him.

"There was a time when I thought I'd go English, too," he said. "I felt so pent up, so caged in…and I just wanted to spread out and have some freedom. I was seventeen, so my *Rumspringa* was well-timed. I was dating a girl named Charity, and one of the things I liked about her was that she wanted that same freedom I did."

"Did you leave?" she asked.

"*Yah*, for about six months," he replied. "And I got a good education in real life. I had to work at minimum wage, pay rent for a room in a shared apartment, and I had the chance to look around at all that freedom. It wasn't quite so wonderful as I thought."

"A lot of Amish teens discover that," she said.

"Well, my girlfriend, Charity, was renting an apartment with some other girls, and when I told her I wanted to go back home again, she didn't," he said. "I tried to convince her to return home, but she was adamant that she couldn't live Amish anymore."

"Oh, Ben…" she breathed.

"You can imagine how that went over when

I came back and I didn't bring Charity with me," he said.

"Yah." Her heart clenched in sympathy. "What did you do?"

"I had to sit down with her *daet* and explain the whole situation. I even brought him with me to the city to talk to her, but she wouldn't be swayed. She was staying."

"And people haven't forgotten," Grace surmised.

"Exactly," he replied. "I'm considered a little bit dangerous now. So there's more to their silly attempts at teaching me how to talk to women. They need me to be better than decent. I have to make up for a lot."

"It isn't fair," she said.

"It's human, though," he countered. For a moment they were both silent, and Grace leaned into Ben's arm. She wanted to comfort him, and maybe even find a little comfort for herself.

"So, you see, I'm attracted to the kind of girl who goes English," Ben said.

Grace swallowed. "Like me?"

"Yah, like you." He smiled faintly. "If it were just a matter of going to another community and finding a wife—well, lots of men do that. Lots of women do, too. But I'm not looking for just a wife."

"Then what do you want?"

"You probably saw couples like this." Ben paused. "Like at a hymn sing, the woman is working hard to help set up the food and drinks, and the man is chatting with friends and setting up chairs. They go through an entire hymn sing and never look at each other once. And if you weren't part of the community—say you were a visitor from out of town—you'd never guess that they were married with five *kinner*."

Grace nodded. "Of course."

"I don't want that." His voice was firm and strong. "I don't want the kind of marriage where you'd need inside information to even know that we belonged together. I want love—the kind the glows out of you. The unmistakable, obvious kind."

"Like Iris and Caleb," she said. "Those two sure seem to glow."

"Yah." He shot her a smile. "Like Iris and Caleb. I want to be the kind of couple that has invisible ties holding them together, even when they're across the room from each other. I want a woman who makes my heart skip a beat."

"That's a big list," she breathed.

"Maybe so," he said. "But I won't be happy with less."

And ironically, neither would she.

"You deserve it, Ben," she said quietly.

He'd found a way back home, and she sincerely hoped he could find the woman who would make his heart skip a beat. Because looking at him in the snow, his gaze turned upward at the night sky, she felt a little rush of longing to be able to do just that.

Ben hadn't meant to say so much. Him and his honesty. He always ended up saying too much. But he had a feeling she needed to hear it—maybe to understand him a little better, but also to grant herself a little forgiveness. She wasn't the only one who'd made life-changing choices.

"It isn't your fault," Grace said. "Charity going English, I mean. It's not your fault that she didn't come home with you."

"I know she had her own choices to make," Ben said.

"She did," Grace said seriously. "For me, it isn't that I wouldn't love to go home, but I've changed too much. I've seen too much. I just can't trust it like I used to, and that isn't my parents' fault, or the community's. They can't blame themselves for what I chose. I was the one who changed."

Ben looked down at her with her hair hanging loose and shining softly in the low light.

"It was my job to take care of her out there," he said.

"It was her job to know what she needed," she replied.

He smiled faintly. "And you think she's better off English?"

Grace was silent for a moment, then shook her head. "I don't know. I think that I'm better off English. I can't speak for anyone else."

Behind them in the house, another peal of laughter echoed out into the cold. He glanced over his shoulder. Someone stood in the window, looking out at them.

"Are you happier?" Ben asked.

Grace shook her head. "Not at all! I was much happier Amish. But I've changed, and even if I want to go back to thinking the way I used to, I can't."

Ben turned toward her. "You were happier Amish?"

She exhaled a slow breath. "I was happier when I believed it would protect me. That I was safe. That is a very cozy feeling."

Did she know how much he wanted to do just that—keep her safe from all the dangers that worried her? And that wasn't just his testosterone-driven ego, either. He didn't feel like this for every woman he came across, but there was something about Grace that sparked it inside of him.

"So, what are you looking for?"

"In life?" she asked.

"*Yah.* What do you hope to find to make all the hard work worth it?"

She smiled faintly. "A husband to love and take care of, some *kinner* of my own, a better chance at staying healthy, and living long enough to see my grandchildren and great-grandchildren, *Gott* willing."

"*Gott* willing," he murmured.

"And do you know what?" she said, turning toward him. "I want a relationship with my family that doesn't depend upon me living Amish. I want to be able to love each other, respect each other, and spend time together without constantly battling over who's right and who's wrong!"

"Because you're wrong, of course," he said, a teasing grin spreading over his face. He couldn't help himself.

"Am I?" she asked, a smile tickling her lips.

"*Yah,*" he said with a short laugh. "The Amish life is better. It's better for you. It's better for all of us. I'm sorry to point it out like that, but you're wrong."

The serious moment wavered and then popped. Grace started to laugh.

"You're rather confident, telling a woman she's wrong." She chuckled. "Just like that."

"It's the confidence that comes with being right."

She bent down and picked up a handful of snow, then lobbed it at his chest. He started to laugh.

"You're worse than my cousin," she said.

He took his own handful of snow and packed it lightly, then tossed it at her a little harder.

"I'm far from your cousin, Grace," he said, catching her gaze and holding it. "Trust me on that."

"Are you so sure?" She picked up more snow and slowly packed it in her hands, watching him with a teasing glint of her own. "He pestered me mercilessly, too."

"Yah," Ben replied. "I'm not your relative, for one. And not only am I right, I'm better at snowball fights. I'm sure of it."

Grace eyed him as if trying to decide what to do, the snow held aloft in her hand. Without warning, she threw the snowball at him, hitting him in the shoulder, where the snow blew apart and sent a cold spray across his cheek.

"You didn't!" he laughed.

"It looks like I did!"

The snowball fight was on, and Ben bent down, picking up another snowball to launch at her. She squealed and ducked, then threw a snowball back that caught him in the stomach.

"I'm a bigger target!" he laughed.

"You're also slower!" she shot back.

"Oh, am I?" He dropped the snow and came toward her, laughing, and it was then that she launched a snowball straight at his face. It exploded against his cheek, and he stopped short in surprise.

She gasped. "I'm sorry! I didn't actually think I'd hit you!"

He blinked, wiping the snow from his face, and when the snow was out of his eyes, he caught her around the waist and tossed her into a soft snowbank. She lay there, her arms and legs akimbo, and her stockings covered in snow. Then she started to laugh, the sound joyful and beautiful—so lovely that it made his heart squeeze.

"Come on," he said, holding out his hand, and Grace reached up for him. He caught her hand and tugged her to her feet, but as she came upright, he found her right in front of him, her lips parted and her eyes shining with laughter.

Neither of them moved, and she inhaled a shaky breath, the smile slipping. Suddenly, Ben couldn't remember what was so funny anymore as his gaze moved over her face.

"Can I just make one point?" he asked, his voice low.

"Sure," she said softly.

"I'm not a cousin or a brother—"

"You're a friend?" she whispered.

"Maybe. But wherever our relationship lands, I'm a man." He pulled off his gloves and reached up to wipe a drop of water from her cheek. She leaned her cheek into his touch ever so slightly, and he stopped there, his hand on her chilled face, their clouded breaths mingling together in the cold air.

He was every inch a man, and whatever this was that had started brewing between them like that sweet coffee latte she'd made, he didn't want her to remember him as anything less. He wasn't a buddy or brother. He might not be a romantic option, either—not realistically. But he was still very much a man.

Grace was so close, so beautiful. Her hair ruffled in the wind, loose and tangled, with some snowflakes clinging in a fringe around her cold-reddened cheeks, and all he could think about were those pink parted lips. So instead of thinking anymore, he dipped his head down and caught her lips with his.

It was like the cold evaporated, and the snow and ice, the house behind, and the stables all disappeared, and it was just the two of them standing there. He dropped his hands to her waist and pulled her gently against him. She leaned into him, her gloved hands catching handfuls of his coat, as his lips moved over hers.

She smelled faintly of cooking from inside, and like something floral that he couldn't quite place. When he pulled back, his breath came out in a rush.

"I didn't plan that," he said softly.

"Me, neither."

He licked his lips, his gaze moving down to her lips once more. But maybe he'd plan this next kiss, and it could all be part of the same mistake. He leaned down again, and she put a hand on his chest, stopping him. He cleared his throat and straightened.

"We shouldn't," she whispered.

No, they shouldn't, but for some reason, it was all he could think about. He swallowed and nodded.

"I'm sorry," he said softly. "But you're incredibly beautiful, and it's easy to forget you aren't Amish."

"Is it?" she asked with a faint smile. "It's easy for me to forget, too."

Behind them, the door opened, and a flood of light spilled out onto the steps. Ben took a purposeful step away from her, and when he turned, he saw his father and Eli in their coats, staring at them in surprise. The Lapps would be heading back to their own farm now—with their own chores to take care of tonight.

"What happened to Grace?" Hannes asked.

Ben looked back at Grace, and for the first time he realized that she was covered in snow. Their eyes met and they both started to laugh.

"We had a snowball fight," Ben said.

"I don't think I won," Grace admitted.

Ben grinned. "I imagine you're cold."

"I'm starting to feel it," she said, her eyes sparkling.

"You'd best head in," he said. "I'll help them hitch up the sleigh."

Grace headed toward the door, and Hannes and Eli came down the steps.

"That is generally not how a young man gets a young lady's attention," Eli joked. "You might have a snowball fight with your sister, but not a pretty young lady like this one."

"Yah, yah," Ben said, rolling his eyes. "I know."

"You could try a compliment, son," Hannes

teased. "You could tell her that she makes a pie as delicious as your own *mamm*'s."

"Or that she sings as sweetly as a morning bird," Eli said.

"That's a good one," Hannes agreed. "Or you could say that she's as fresh as a morning in May."

"That's a good one, too!" Eli said. "I used that with Irene, I'll have you know."

"*Yah*, I used it with my Ruth, too," Hannes said, and the older men nodded sagely.

"Or you could tell her that her needlework is so neat that you'd think it was bought in a store," Eli said, turning back to Ben.

Ben cast Eli and Hannes an amused look. Yes, the old men thought they were experts in wooing women. And maybe they had been, a good many years ago, when it had come to the women they married.

But snowball fight or not, Ben had just kissed Grace under that silken moonlight, and the memory of her slim form under layers of clothes and her breath tickling his face still warmed his blood.

Maybe it had been badly timed, and it had been with a woman who wasn't staying, and who he had no right to think about more than friendship with, but he'd meant that kiss. If things were different—if Grace could find a way back to the faith, or if they'd met properly at a hymn sing, or at someone's harvest— he would be asking her out for a drive and talking rather seriously about the future.

If things were different...

"You could compliment her thriftiness with money!" Hannes was saying.

"Or her way with *kinner*...good practice for a family of her own," Eli added, and Ben stifled a smile.

But things weren't different. And this kiss would have to be the end of it.

Chapter Eleven

That night, after the family was asleep, and little Taylor was slumbering peacefully in her cradle, Grace lay in her bed fully awake, her heart in turmoil. Before getting into bed, she'd looked outside the window and saw the wind blowing over the snow, whisking it up into low clouds that scuttled across the fields. It blew off the roof of the stable—powdery crystals that sparkled in the moonlight.

Grace got up and sat in a chair next to the cold window, a quilt from her bed wrapped around her shoulders, watching the quiet beauty outside. But her mind wasn't on the scene below. She was still remembering that kiss. It had been both wildly unprofessional and wonderful at the same time. She could re-member exactly how it felt—his lips on hers, his breath warming her face, his strength. She saw the exact spot where it had happened—the perfect expanse of snow broken from where they'd laughed and thrown snowballs.

That had been her first kiss.

Funny—she'd wondered what her first kiss might be like, and she'd never imagined it happening so unexpectedly. When she was an Amish teen, she'd thought it might happen on a buggy ride, going home from singing. In her English life, she'd wondered if perhaps a nice young man would drop her back off at her apartment and kiss her at the threshold. She'd seen those kisses in movies and on TV shows. She thought she knew how it was supposed to happen.

But she'd never gotten to that point in a relationship with any man before, Amish or English. Now that it had happened, it was with a man she could never be with. And that made her heart ache in a way she'd never felt before. But that kiss… Her stomach still fluttered at the memory.

Grace rubbed her hands over her face and stood up, tugging the quilt closer around her torso to keep the warmth in. Iris was snoring softly, and the entire house was still. Taylor's soother made soft *nuk-nuk* sounds as she sucked in her sleep. Grace crept out of the room, pulling the door shut behind her with a soft *click*, and moved through the dark hallway.

The cold floorboards creaked under her bare feet, and she slipped down the stairs, away from the sleeping family. She didn't know what she wanted to do—just get some time alone, process, think.

The kitchen was silent, moonlight spilling in through the windows and pooling on the wooden floor. An Amish kitchen was so much different from an English one. Friends had commented on her kitchen—how she kept it clean and neatly organized.

"It's like a farmhouse kitchen, right in the middle of the city!" one friend had exclaimed. "That's what it is!"

Her Amish roots, while she didn't talk about them, influenced everything from her simple home decor to her aversion to flower-patterned prints on her clothes. Her Amish way of thinking had made her socially awkward when it came to English relationships, and had kept her shy when it came to getting to know men.

Her Amish roots had held her back. At least that was what she'd thought, time and time again, when she fumbled uncomfortably to make conversation during a coffee date with a man who'd seemed promising.

And yet, there was a little whisper of wisdom that came from that Amish upbringing.

Gott doesn't make mistakes, her mother had always said. *He is in each detail, if we only look for Him.*

Was *Gott* in this storm? Was He in this strange, snowed-in visit with an Amish family that made her lonesome for all she'd given up? Was He in this strange situation with an abandoned baby that needed love so badly?

Her *mamm* would say decidedly yes. She believed that *Gott* could redeem the mess and put it right again.

But Tabitha was dead. There was no making that right again. And Grace's eyes had been opened to bigger issues, deeper problems, and dangers she'd never imagined before. That couldn't be undone.

Grace tiptoed through the kitchen and into the sitting room. As a child, she used to find her mother praying on her knees, her elbows resting on the couch cushions, and suddenly she had an overwhelming urge to do just that.

Grace needed answers, not platitudes. She needed clear guidance. She needed comfort… and while she'd found that with *Gott* even out with the *Englishers,* she needed it even more tonight.

So Grace sank to her knees on the rag rug

and folded her hands, resting her elbows on the couch cushions like her mother had. Kneeling here, it was like all the extra things that weighed her down slipped away, and she was left with two things that filled up her aching heart—her loneliness for her family and this tall, handsome man who sparked emotions inside of her that she dared not explore. She let her eyes close as she opened her heart.

Gott, *why did you bring me here?* she prayed. *Why did you trap me here, snow me in with this perfectly lovely family? You know who I am! You know why I left, and I still believe You were leading me when I did.*

I couldn't stay and risk my health, all in order to trust a system. I'm supposed to trust You! And I'm doing that. I'm trying. You've shown me a world I hardly understood, and You've allowed me to help countless people in my profession. I am blessed, and I am grateful.

Her heart ached, all the same.

And I am so, so lonely...

Her feelings and her thoughts tumbled out as she poured them out before her Maker. She needed guidance, and answers, and direction, and reassurance... She needed to know the next step, because up until this snowed-in visit, she'd been very sure about the direction her life was taking.

Even if it was hard being English, she'd been helping make a difference.

Even if she was lonely in the English world, she still had *Gott*.

Grace wasn't sure how long she knelt there, opening her heart to *Gott*, but when a sound behind her roused her, she lifted her head and turned. Ben stood in the doorway, dressed in a pair of pants and a long-sleeved thermal undershirt.

"I didn't mean to disturb you," he whispered. His hair was rumpled, and there was the softest shadow of whiskers across his chin.

Grace pushed herself to her feet, and her knees ached a little from a long time in the same position. "It's okay."

"You were praying," he said.

"*Yah*... My mother used to pray early in the morning in the sitting room, and—" She smiled faintly. "I'm starting to understand why."

"Worry?" he asked.

"A little," she admitted.

Ben came into the room and sat on the edge of the armchair across from her. He leaned forward, resting his elbows on his knees.

"Am I the cause of any of this worry?" he asked, his voice low and deep. "I kissed you, and…" He cleared his throat. "Did I upset you?"

Grace felt her cheeks heat. "No, it wasn't that. I mean—" She pressed her hands together. "My parents assumed that when I went English it was on my own, in rebellion, in spite of *Gott*'s leading. But that wasn't true. When I left, I had prayed for weeks. I knew it was the right thing to do and that things had to change in our community, or women wouldn't be safe. We couldn't make decisions for ourselves when it came to seeing a doctor. If I stayed, and just followed the rules in front of me, nothing would ever change. It wasn't right to close my eyes."

"So you felt that *Gott* wanted you to leave?" Ben asked. She could see the disbelief in his dark gaze.

"You don't think that's possible," she said.

"The Amish way is *Gott*'s will," Ben said. "In a sinful world filled with secular passions competing for people's attention, the Amish life keeps us focused on what matters most."

"And yet, we need the *Englishers*," she pointed out. "We can't survive without them. They buy our wares and they provide us with so much more. Their army protects this American soil. Their elections provide leaders to govern. Their doctors and hospitals provide us with medical care—and that doesn't happen on an eighth-grade education. We need their sewage systems, even. We need their police to protect us from criminals. Ben, we even wait on their snowplows! How can an English life be so wicked when we rely upon them so much?"

Ben nodded. "I know the arguments. I had a *Rumspringa*, too."

She felt the dismissal in those words, but it wasn't spiritual immaturity that had taken her out of the Amish world.

"You were joking before about you being right and me being wrong, but I felt *Gott*'s leading when I left my family home, Ben," she said. "And forgive the rudeness, but I don't need you to believe it for me to know it's true."

Ben's eyes widened in surprise.

"I'm sorry," he said. "I didn't mean to sound flippant."

She nodded. "It's okay."

"It's just…not the first assumption someone makes when someone jumps the fence—that it's for the best," he said.

"It's possible for *Gott* to lead people in different directions," she said. "*Gott* led

Abraham on a journey, but He didn't take everyone. *Gott* brought Joseph to Egypt all by himself and brought him through trial after trial for His own purposes. Sometimes *Gott* has a journey for someone that takes them away from home."

"And this was yours," Ben said quietly.

"*Yah*, I do believe this has been mine," she said. "I don't think it was a mistake."

"Even if it hurts," he murmured. "Even if you miss the Amish life."

"That's why I'm praying," she whispered, and tears prickled in her eyes. "I'm needing some guidance."

He smiled faintly. "I'll pray that you get it."

Grace sucked in a slow breath. She needed *Gott* to tell her the next step, the right choice, because she couldn't see it for herself. It was like groping in the dark and having a lamp that only showed her the very next step. It would be easier if she could see ahead, see the pitfalls, the outcomes…but *Gott* didn't give that kind of clarity. He gave a small kerosene lamp.

Outside, Grace heard the far-off growl of an engine. Both she and Ben instinctively turned toward the window, and the sound moved closer, combined with the scraping sound of metal against road. Ben stepped closer to her to get a better view out the window.

For a moment, they were motionless. Then Ben's fingers closed over hers, and the gesture was such a welcome one that she leaned into his strong arm.

A yellow snowplow came into view, crawling down the road at the speed of a trotting buggy, snow billowing up beside it in the illumination of headlights.

"They're clearing the roads," Ben said.

Those *Englisher* snowplows that even the Amish relied upon to clear the way for life to get back to its regular rhythm. It wasn't quite so simple as good and evil, right and wrong. But it had been so much easier when that was all she'd seen.

"Yah," Grace said, tightening her grip on Ben's strong hand.

The snow that had locked her in with this family, with this all-too-handsome man at her side, was being pushed out of the way, providing her an exit.

"It looks like you'll leave tomorrow," Ben said.

"Yes," she said in English. "I have a report to write and a baby girl to bring in to the office."

Ben squeezed her hand and then released it.

"We'd best get to bed, then," he said, his dark gaze meeting hers miserably. "Morning won't wait on us."

"Yah..." she breathed. "I suppose we should."

This little respite from her regular English life was soon to be over. This time with a handsome man, an unexpected romance she'd hardly even admit to, was going to end.

Ben turned and headed out of the sitting room. She heard one creak on the stairs, and then all was silent again.

Tomorrow, she'd be heading back to the life *Gott* had led her to. Away from Redemption. Away from Ben.

Why did that hurt?

The next morning, Ben finished his chores earlier than usual. Hannes was feeling much better, and they worked together to muck out horse stalls and take care of the barn. When they were done, they went inside for breakfast.

Ben hadn't seen Grace yet that morning since he'd gone out earlier than usual, and when he came into the warm kitchen, he stopped short. Grace stood by the counter wearing her plum-colored pantsuit. Her hair was twisted up at the back of her head, secured with a golden-colored clip, and when she turned, it was like a gulf had opened up between them.

She was English again. *So* English.

"Good morning," he said. His voice sounded different in his own ears, too.

"Morning." She smiled. "We have some fresh coffee."

"That would be great."

He accepted a mug of coffee, passed it to his father and then took the next one she handed to him.

"So you're leaving this morning," he said.

"Just as soon as the drive is cleared," she said, and he saw the sadness swimming in her eyes, too.

"*Yah*, I'll get started right after breakfast," he said.

She didn't answer, and he didn't blame her. They had an audience between them, and while there was so much he wanted to say, he couldn't.

After he'd finished eating, Ben hitched their two biggest quarter horses up to the plow and set about the lengthy work of plowing out their drive. Normally this was a chore that was soothing. But today, it felt like each pass he made, plowing the snow out of the way, clearing a path, he was coming closer to a final goodbye.

Grace hadn't been here long—only a few days—but somehow it felt like he'd known her longer. Maybe it was the storm, but the time together had been deeper, more revealing, more emotionally intense. And he wished they could keep going like this—talking, working, stealing some kisses… As if that process wouldn't tear his heart into pieces given any amount of time.

Grace had been awfully clear last night. *Gott* had led her to the *Englishers*, as unbelievable to him as that might be. And she was going back.

As Ben reined the horses in at the start of the drive, just beside the stables, he heard a car's engine, and he turned to see a police car pulling into the drive. He dismounted from the plow and waited until the patrol car came to a stop. The door opened, and an officer in his uniform blues stepped out.

"Hello, is this this Hochstetler farm?" the officer asked.

"Yah," Ben said. "I'm Ben Hochstetler."

"I'm Officer Aiden Hank," he replied. "This is my partner, Officer Chris Nelson." The other officer got out, as well.

Ben nodded a hello to each of them.

"Did you call for social services before the storm hit?" Officer Hank asked. "Because a social services agent named Grace Schweitzer was dispatched out here, and her office hasn't heard from her."

"*Yah*, we did call," Ben said. "And she arrived. There was a baby dropped on our doorstep, and she came to pick her up. Then the storm started to blow, and she couldn't safely leave. She's inside the house."

"Really glad to hear that." A smile broke over the officer's face. "Do you mind?" He hooked a thumb toward the house, and Ben nodded.

"Of course not," Ben said. "Come inside."

Ben led the way through the door. The house still smelled of breakfast cooking. Iris was at the sink doing dishes, and Hannes sat at the kitchen table, a wire mesh basket of eggs in front of him. Grace stood by the counter, Taylor up on her shoulder with a burp cloth as she gently patted the infant's back. Everyone looked up in surprise when the officers came in. Grace's gaze flickered toward Ben, and even though he knew he had no right to it, he felt a surge of protectiveness toward her. She wasn't his to guard, but tell his heart that this morning.

"Grace Schweitzer?" Officer Nelson asked.

"Yes, I'm Grace," she said with a hesitant smile. "Is everything okay?"

"It is now," Officer Nelson replied. "Your office called you in as missing, and we were all hoping you'd made it this far before that storm closed in."

"Yes, I've been well cared for," she said. Her gaze flickered toward Ben again, and he felt his chest tighten.

Officer Hank pushed a button on his radio and relayed the fact that they'd found her to the police dispatch.

"They'll let your office know ASAP," he said once he released the button.

"Thank you," Grace said.

"This is the baby?" Officer Hank tipped his head to one side and smiled down at her. "I have a daughter this age."

"Iris, would you grab the note the mother left?" Grace asked.

"I can get that," Ben said. He knew where it was, on the counter next to a basket of apples. He passed it over to the officer, who opened it and read it.

"We found the mother," Officer Nelson said. "She came to the local police during the storm. She was frantic. She said she'd left her baby at an Amish farm, and she wanted to go back for her. But there was no way she was getting through."

"Do you know anything about the mother?" Grace asked. "Is she Amish, for example?"

"I don't know," Officer Nelson replied. "I didn't see her, personally."

Grace was moving back into her English role—Ben could see it happening, almost physically. She was holding herself differently now, her voice full of authority. She was part of a team with these officers who would deal with the problem of the abandoned baby.

"Are you okay to get back to the city on your own?" Officer Nelson asked.

"Yes. I made sure my car would start yesterday, so I'll be fine getting Taylor here back to my office. I'm set with a car seat and everything I'll need."

"Glad to hear it," he replied. "I'll radio in and tell them that you're on your way, then."

Ben watched the exchange in silence, and when the officers took their leave, he shook their hands in farewell and shut the door behind them. This was it. Grace was leaving. She had a job to do.

"So they found the young mother," Hannes said thoughtfully.

Ben came back into the kitchen, and he scrubbed a hand through his hair.

"I should make sure the car will start again," Grace said.

"I'll help you with that," Ben said. Even though he knew nothing about cars, it might be the last chance he had to talk to her alone.

"Why don't I take over with the *bobbily*?" Hannes said, giving Ben an understanding look. "You two do what you need to."

Those last words felt loaded, and when his father took the baby, he wondered how much Hannes had guessed about his feelings for Grace. Maybe it didn't matter anymore. He wasn't going to be able to hide it.

"I'll be sad to see this little one go," Iris said. "I've gotten attached."

So had Ben, to be honest, but it was to more than the baby in the house. His feelings were in a jumble of painful tugs and longings. But he'd see Grace off, say a proper goodbye, and then do some chores and pick out that knot of emotion alone.

Grace put on her fitted woolen coat over her pantsuit, and Ben followed her outside.

"What's the matter?" Grace asked when she caught his gaze on her.

"You look English again," he admitted.

She licked her lips. "I am English, Ben."

"Not all the way," he said. "Not as English as you look."

Her cheeks flushed, and he wondered if he'd angered her. She opened the car door and slid into the driver's seat. The engine rumbled to life. When she emerged from the car once more, she straightened.

"Ben, I know that we talked about this, and you don't see anything wrong with the way our friendship grew while I was here, but—" she let out a shaky breath "—my boss would think differently. The way I acted here, getting closer to you than I should have, that would be seen as incredibly unprofessional. It would be discipline-worthy at my office, as a matter of fact, and I feel I owe you an apology."

"I said it before, and I'll say it again…" He felt his irritation starting to rise. "Whatever has developed between us is something honest, and I won't have it picked apart by your boss or anyone else."

"Thank you." She dropped her gaze.

"You were here because *Gott* snowed you in, Grace," he said frankly. "That storm wasn't expected in this area—not like that. *Gott* is in the details, and He brought you here."

"Maybe," she agreed.

Definitely, but he wasn't going to argue about that. "I'll miss you."

"Me, too," she said, and she smiled sadly.

"Maybe you could come back and visit,"

he said hopefully. "Then this wouldn't be a goodbye."

"You won't be here, remember?" she asked softly. "Your sister will be newly married, you'll be off finding a wife in Shipshewana, and when you do return, I have a feeling your new-bride won't be very pleased to see me."

A new bride. The idea no longer held any appeal to him...not if he had to marry someone else. His heart was taken, and he wasn't going to be much use to another woman, no matter how sweet she might be.

"I don't want to go to Shipshewana," he said.

"Ben—" Her breath hung in the air.

"Grace, I'm serious," he said, shaking his head. "This is what I was looking for, and waiting for, and why I was driving everyone crazy because I said I could find it, and they didn't believe me."

"This?" she asked hesitantly.

"You." Was she going to force him to say it? She stared at him mutely, so he plunged on. "I don't know what it is about you, but I feel like I've known you for years. And I know I haven't. It's just, with you, I—" he cast about for the words "—I feel like myself. I can open up about what I think. And when I see you, my heart beats differently."

"That might be a medical condition," she murmured, and she smiled faintly.

"Teasing?" he said with a low laugh. "When I'm pouring my heart out to you?"

"Ben, you don't mean it."

"I do mean it!" He sobered. "Do you think I'd say all this for nothing? Grace, I wanted a woman who I'd fall for, hat over boots, and I fell for you. Was it stupid? Very! Was it planned? Not a chance. None of this makes sense. None of it is easy. But it's *honest*."

"Are you sure it wasn't just the storm?"

"If it was, it's a storm that *Gott* brought in," he said. "It wasn't *just* a storm. When I kissed you, did you feel something?"

Grace's breath came quick and shallow. He stepped closer, pulled off his gloves and ran a finger down her cheek. She leaned into his touch again like she had when he kissed her, and he wanted to kiss her again, block out all this pain and find some relief in her arms.

"Tell me you felt nothing, and I'll never mention it again," he whispered.

"I…felt something," she said. "Of course I did. I don't go around kissing men for nothing. In fact, I've never kissed a man before."

"What?" He frowned, searching her face for more joking. "You mean I'm the first to kiss you?"

She shrugged faintly, her expression hesitant. Well, if he was the first to kiss her, let him do it again, and if nothing else, she'd always remember him. He pulled her into his arms, and she tipped her face up, meeting his anguished gaze. When she didn't pull away, he lowered his lips over hers. She leaned into his embrace, and he let the world around him disappear. His family might very well be watching from the window, and he didn't care.

When he pulled back, her eyes fluttered open.

"You shouldn't play with feelings like these," she whispered.

"Playing?" he said incredulously, his voice coming out gruff past the lump in his throat. "I'm not playing! I love you, Grace."

He let her go, and she took an unsteady step back.

Their relationship was fast, he knew. It was shocking, even to himself, but it was also true. He didn't need a barn or an empty field or chores to sort out these jumbled feelings anymore. They were lined up in an orderly fashion, clear as day—he loved her.

Chapter Twelve

Grace's heart hammered hard in her chest, and her gloved hands fluttered up to her lips. His words were still settling in, and her brain was spinning to catch up.

"What?" she breathed.

Ben lifted his shoulders helplessly. "It's the truth."

He loved her. Just like that. It was the kind of romance she'd been waiting for—the kind that fell together and just made sense...the kind that had started to feel like an impossibility! But it was with the wrong man. He was Amish. He knew exactly what he wanted. And she'd never be a comfortable Amish woman again.

"You...love me?" Was she just being a glutton for punishment, wanting to hear it again?

"*Yah*, Grace, I love you," he said softly.

"It wasn't planned, and it makes no sense—I know it. But I love you, and I couldn't let you leave without at least telling you."

He needed a sweet woman in an apron and *kapp*, who trusted the *Ordnung* and the men in church leadership to want what was best for her. He needed a woman who believed in this way of life just as ardently as he did. He didn't need *her*!

"I'm not Amish anymore, and I'm not the kind of woman you need, Ben."

"I know."

"What you need is to go to Shipshewana and find a nice woman who wants to live Amish," she said. "That will give you a happy life!"

"I know that, too," he said with a shake of his head.

"Then why tell me you love me?" she demanded. "Do you know what that does to me?"

"It isn't that I don't see the logic of going to find a good Amish woman," Ben said. "It's that my heart won't listen. I've always had this yearning for exactly this…this unexplainable connection you and I share. I want love—passion, a commitment that doesn't come from vows, but from a place deep inside of both of us that just won't let go! I want a real, deep love."

Grace was silent. Because so did she. She wanted exactly that, and she'd been praying for it for years…but not like this. She'd been praying for that one enigma of an *Englisher* man who would embrace her as the Amish-born rebel she was. She'd prayed for an *Englisher.*

"Is that over the top?" Ben asked miserably.

Grace shook her head. "It's perfect. It's what I want, too, but our feelings can't be enough here. You have to see that."

"I'm not stupid," Ben said. "I know this is terrible for me, but I didn't exactly have a choice here. I fell in love with you."

"But you have a choice *now*," she insisted.

Neither of them had to do this. They could straighten their shoulders and walk away— couldn't they? Couldn't *he*?

"You said you felt something, too," Ben pressed. "Tell me I'm not a fool who's feeling this alone."

What did Grace feel for him? It was a mixture of admiration, respect, tenderness and a ridiculously unfounded hope that she might see him again somehow, some way…that she could fall into his arms and just stay there.

"I think…" Grace said softly. "I think that I've fallen in love with you, too, Ben."

Ben nodded twice, and his Adam's apple bobbed up and down.

"This is a good thing." He tugged her closer, and she resisted the urge to lean into those strong arms.

"No, it isn't!" she said.

"It's better than just me falling boots over hat for an *Englisher*," Ben said. "That would mean there was something seriously wrong with me. But if you're feeling what I am, then—"

"Then what?" she demanded. "Then we're both miserable? Because you need an Amish woman who understands you, and I need an *Englisher* man who can embrace the Amish in me. We're the opposite of what each other needs!"

"Maybe there's a way," he said.

"How?" She shook her head. "Are you going to come English with me? Find a job, finish high school, make a life with me?"

His expression clouded. "You know I can't do that."

And even though she hadn't expected otherwise, the words stung.

"I do know it," she admitted. "But, Ben, I'm not Amish. You won't accept that. I was raised Amish, but I'm not Amish *anymore*. I can't trust it! The *Ordnung* is beautiful when everything is working the way it should, when people are healthy and we aren't surprised by calamity. But I'm not sure I can trust it with my *life*."

Ben didn't say anything.

"We're worlds apart," she whispered.

"Are you sure you don't see yourself in a *kapp* and apron, some *kinner* running through the house and a devoted husband coming home to you?" he asked.

The image was so beautiful that it nearly cracked her in two. She longed for exactly that—to be needed, to be loved, to be a part of a bustling family again. But that image of family harmony wasn't necessarily how things would go. What if she ended up in a hospital bed, fighting for her life because she trusted that beautiful picture to never change?

"Oh, I can imagine that family," she said, her voice wavering with suppressed tears. "It's perfect in every way. And maybe that's the problem, because life isn't perfect. Life is infinitely harder than those beautiful pictures, Ben. I know it because of what happened to my sister, and I know it from my work with social services. Life is *hard*."

Ben pulled his hat off and rubbed a hand through his hair.

"There is no way, is there?" he asked, and his voice caught.

She shook her head. "There's no way..."

Even though she wished with all her heart that there was. But with the Amish, there was no halfway. There was the narrow path, and the road to destruction. There was no comfortably paved side street available to them.

"What if I don't bring a wife home?" he asked. "Will you come visit me then?"

Grace shook her head. "Don't do that for me, Ben. Get married. Have that houseful of *kinner.* You deserve it."

And she deserved to find a good *Englisher* man, too. They both deserved love that would fill their hearts...with other people.

Ben swallowed, his eyes misting.

"I'll miss you all the same," he said gruffly.

"Me, too." She could hardly hold her tears back anymore, and she looked toward the house. Iris and Hannes were in the window, and when they saw that she'd spotted them, they startled and pulled back.

"I have to bring Taylor back to the office," she said.

Ben nodded. "I know."

Grace pulled open the car door and slipped

into the driver's seat just long enough to turn on the heat and got out again. It was time to go back. Maybe she'd be able to think straight again once she got away from this man who made her feel too much, and this farm that reminded her too much of home.

Ben stood back, and she headed up to the house. She let herself in and found Iris and Hannes both staring at her, eyes wide, expressions uncertain.

"I just need to get Taylor into the car seat," Grace said, fighting back tears. "And I want to thank you for taking such good care of her...and for your hospitality. I truly appreciate it."

The words were not enough, and she'd likely think of much better ways to say it while she drove away from this little Amish farm. Right now, though, with her heart cracking in her chest, it was the best she could do.

"It was very nice to get to know you," Iris said. "I'd love it if you came to my wedding."

"I won't be able to." Grace leaned in and gave Iris a quick squeeze. "But I wish you a lifetime of happiness with Caleb. You are a beautiful couple."

Hannes brought the baby over, and Grace settled her into the car seat, doing up the buckles and adjusting them so that they were just right. The baby looked up at her with those searching, dark blue eyes, and Grace tucked the blankets around her.

"Wait—" Iris left the room and came back with a quilt. "Take this with her. It will be warmer."

Grace accepted it with a misty smile. "Thank you. For everything."

"I made up an extra bottle," Hannes said, handing it over. "And, young lady—"

Grace turned back to the older man, wondering what he'd say. Had he seen that kiss outside? Was this going to be a reprimand?

"My son is a good man," Hannes said quietly. "He told us that your *mamm* in Creekside is praying for you to come back to the faith, and I just want to let you know that our prayers are joining hers. We would love to see you again, Grace Schweitzer. You have friends here."

Grace felt a tear slip down her cheek. He meant well. She knew that his prayers came from a place of goodness and love inside of him, and she held her hand out to shake his.

"Thank you, Hannes," she said. "It is comforting to be in a good man's prayers."

She quickly wiped the tear from her cheek. She was a professional, after all, and while this visit had become incredibly personal, she had to get herself back under control. She gathered up the car seat, bottle and bag of diapers, and waited while Hannes opened the door for her. She headed back out to the car.

"Goodbye," she said. "And thank you again."

Ben was waiting for her. He helped her load everything inside the car, and he waited while she finished clipping the car seat into the base. Taylor's eyes were getting heavy, and Grace touched her soother to make sure it stayed in her mouth. Then she shut the back door.

"Is this goodbye, then?" he asked.

"Yah." She nodded. Then she put her hand in her pocket and felt one of her business cards there. She wouldn't come back to visit, but if Ben ever found himself questioning the Amish life like she had, she wanted him to be able to find her. She pulled it out and handed it over. "If you ever need me…"

He accepted the card and looked down at it. Then he stepped back, and she got into her car.

She turned the car around and glanced over to find Hannes and Iris standing at the open door and Ben's agonized gaze locked on her vehicle.

As she drove up the freshly plowed drive

and turned onto the road, she felt like she was leaving the last of her Amish self behind on that little farm. For years, she'd been holding herself in a strange balance between two worlds—the Amish upbringing she never spoke of and the English life she was determined to live.

Was this what she needed—a final chance to say goodbye to the Amish world? Because she could have had all of it—the loving husband, the big family, the children of her own—and she'd turned it down. She'd made her choice all over again.

Was this what she'd needed? And if so, why did her heart feel like it was breaking?

The road was long and straight, and there was a horse-drawn buggy coming up in the distance. She couldn't drive with tears blurring her vision like this, so she pulled over to the side of the road, put on her hazards and let her forehead drop to the top of her steering wheel. There she let the tears overtake her, and she sobbed out her grief. She was crying for all she'd given up when she'd left Creekside, her parents and her younger siblings. She was crying for the stretched, misshapen life she led that was never fully hers. And she cried for the man she'd fallen in love with, the man she couldn't marry and couldn't make happy.

Was this what *Gott* had wanted from her—this gut-wrenching sacrifice?

"Hello? Hello?" a voice called.

She looked up, wiping her eyes. The buggy had stopped, and the bearded Amish man looked at her through the window with concern. She lowered her window and blinked back her tears.

"Yes?" she said in English.

"Are you all right?" he asked. "Do you need help?"

"I'm fine. Thank you, though," she said, and she forced a shaky smile. She closed the window and put the car into gear.

She needed to get this baby girl back to Vaughnville. And if Taylor was an Amish baby, here was hoping that this child was less conflicted and torn about her roots than Grace was.

That night, the air warmed considerably. It went from a deep freeze to almost balmy in comparison. The outdoor thermometer hovered right above the freezing mark. But the air felt even warmer than that to Ben, and he undid his coat as he worked, letting some cooling air in.

The blizzard was past, and the snow was melting off the tree limbs, dropping in wet chunks to the ground. The icicles were dripping, and Ben was glad that they'd shoveled off the house roof when they had, because the snow would be heavy right now, and all that water would need a place to go. Like the tears inside of him—locked in, threatening.

When the rest of his chores were done, Ben headed out to the barn. He hadn't slept well. In fact, he hadn't gone to bed until nearly midnight, and this morning he'd woken up ragged and worn out.

Grace was gone.

Grace had only been with them a few days, so it didn't stand to reason that she'd seep into the wood grain around here. But she had...at least for Ben. The house felt a little emptier without her and the baby in it.

Iris had breakfast ready when Ben and Hannes finished with the stable. The task had gone a lot slower because they had to shovel snow away from doors, break the ice in the water trough and let the horses back outside again, all before they mucked out stalls.

Iris had plans to spend time with Irene Lapp that day. They were going to do some sewing and cooking and just enjoying each other's company before the wedding. Iris was anxious for her big day, and she wasn't paying much attention to her brother's emotional state, which was a relief. This was something Ben would work through on his own.

His father, on the other hand, was a little more difficult to shake. There was a large amount of work waiting for them in the barn, and as they trudged through the softening, wet snow after breakfast, Ben couldn't help but wonder what was happening with Grace.

"She might come back," Hannes said.

Ben looked over at his father, startled out of his own thoughts. "What?"

"She knows where to find you," Hannes said. "Maybe she'll come back."

"She knows I'm going to Shipshewana to find a wife," he replied.

"*Yah*, but you haven't gone yet."

And there was no saying he'd be successful, especially if his heart was no longer in it. The problem had always been that he knew what he was looking for on a heart level, and finding it wasn't easy. Now that he'd found it with the least appropriate woman possible, he wasn't going to be able to make do with anything less.

"*Daet*, we said all we needed to say yesterday. She's not Amish anymore, no matter how Amish she seems in a dress. She's just…not."

And that was the part that hurt the most, because he'd connected with her on that level—with her in an Amish cape dress and cooking in his kitchen. Even with her hair down around her shoulders, she still seemed to belong in an Amish home.

Had he just been fooling himself? Were his feelings for her only for one side of her life? She was a whole woman, and her experiences weren't confined to her Amish upbringing, but he couldn't join her on the other side of the fence. It was impossible.

If he were smart, he'd start the process of letting her go.

And he'd find a nice woman and try to make do.

Ben sighed. He wasn't very good at being an Amish man, either. He didn't sacrifice his own hopes and desires very easily, even if it was for the Amish life he was devoted to.

Hannes looked up at the barn roof as they approached the building. A chunk of wet snow slid off the roof and fell with a heavy splat a couple of yards to their left. Hannes shaded his eyes and took a few steps back to see better.

"That's a lot of snow," Hannes said.

"*Yah*, it sure is," Ben said.

Ben pulled open the barn door, and they

both headed inside. Besides the usual sounds of the goats, the calves and a couple of milk cows, there was the unsettling sound of dripping water.

"We've got a leaking roof," Hannes said. "I knew we should have replaced it this summer."

"*Yah*, but with the broken wagon, and all that hail damage to the windows, we didn't have anything extra," Ben replied.

"True." Hannes headed in the direction of the drip, and he looked up, squinting. "There it is. Oh, my… Look at that roof sag!"

Hannes was right—the roof was literally bulging under the wet weight of that snow. Ordinarily, it would have slid off on its own, but with a concave spot to hold it, all it did was melt and get wetter, heavier.

"Eli and Caleb will help us replace that section," Hannes said. "I'm sure Noah, Thomas and Amos would lend a hand, too."

"*Yah*," Ben agreed. "They will."

This was what the community was for— helping each other when times were hard, when storms blew and roofs failed. There was obligation to each other, but also the warmth of friendship. What did the *Englishers* do when times got hard? Was it just insurance money that cushioned them? Or people hired in social services to step in when times were hardest? Didn't they yearn for something with a little more heart behind it?

Because he did...and it was one heart in particular that he couldn't stop thinking about.

"Even Steve Mills," Hannes said.

Steve—the *Englisher* down the road who could be counted on like any Amish man—willing to lend a hand, a horse or a few hours of labor.

"You know, I bet with Steve and Eli, we could get this fixed in a day," Hannes said thoughtfully.

Steve had a telephone when they needed it and a full toolbox that he was happy to put to use in the aid of a neighbor. He wasn't Amish or even Anabaptist. He was Pentecostal and as different from them as cats and chickens. But Christian. Deeply Christian. And something suddenly snapped together in Ben's mind, the connections making sense. Why hadn't he seen this before?

"Do you know why I trust him?" Ben asked.

"Who, Steve?" his father asked.

"*Yah*—it's because he prays, and somehow whenever we need a hand, *Gott* sends Steve down the road in our direction. A man who prays—you aren't counting on the man. You're counting on the One he talks to."

Hannes lifted his eyebrows. "*Yah*, I could see that."

Ben nodded slowly, but an idea had started to bloom inside of him. Sometimes a man had to know Who he was trusting—*Gott* or a human being. People could let a man down, but *Gott* was faithful.

And a woman who prayed, who could be found on her knees in the middle of the night, was a woman in contact with the right Source.

"*Daet*, I'm going up to the roof, and I'll clear off as much of that snow as I can," Ben said. "And then I'm heading down to Steve's place and asking him to help us out." Ben eyed his father for a moment. "I'm also going to ask to use his phone."

"Are you calling Grace?" Hannes asked, a smile tickling at the corners of his lips.

"I'm calling a taxi," he said. "There are some things a man needs to ask a woman face to face, and this is one of them. But I'll be back this evening, and I'll work every waking hour tomorrow to finish up that stretch of roof."

Hannes eyed him for a moment, then nodded.

"She's not Amish, son," the older man said soberly.

"No, *Daet*, but the woman prays like you

wouldn't believe. And I don't know how to explain, but I can trust that prayer…you know?"

Hannes chewed on the side of his cheek, then shrugged. "*Gott* is the one we can trust, son. I'll give you that. I'll start the milking and feed the calves if you want to get snow off that part of the roof."

There was always work to be done, but Ben's heart felt lighter as he went in search of a shovel and a ladder. There were neighbors for tough times, but the One they trusted with their hearts and their future didn't live down the road or have a field that butted against theirs. The One they trusted most was the One who created them.

And while Ben had no idea what *Gott* was up to, he knew that *Gott* didn't make mistakes, and He was in the details of an untimely blizzard and a baby on the doorstep.

Sometimes, after all seemed lost, *Gott*'s voice was in the steady drip of a leaking roof.

Chapter Thirteen

Grace arrived at the office the next morning with a heavy heart. She'd hoped that getting back to work would somehow erase the emotional upheaval of the last few days, but it hadn't worked out that way. Lying in bed last night, she'd cried. There was no solution. She'd left her heart with a man who needed so much more than she had to offer. Or perhaps he just needed a woman with less baggage, less heartbreak, fewer lessons learned the hard way.

Where were the love and family that she'd been praying for all these years? It would be easier to visit her parents with a dapper *Englisher* husband at her side, someone to give her emotional support and remind her that her choices hadn't been wrong.

But she'd never met him. And the girls

she'd grown up with in Creekside were all married now with babies of their own. Life had marched on for all of them, but somehow for Grace, it had gotten into a rut.

When she came into the office that morning, she had a very special case to deal with— the young mother who had abandoned her baby. Her name was Abigail Ebersole, and she wasn't *exactly* Amish, but she was very young…

Grace sat in a chair across from the teenaged mother, who cradled Taylor in her arms. Tears had left the girl's eyes puffy and her cheeks moist. She pressed a kiss against the baby's head.

"Can you tell me what happened, Abigail?" Grace asked softly.

Taylor had gone to a temporary foster home the night before. Abigail had some time with her daughter yesterday, some time with a psychiatrist, and then the baby was taken for the night for cautionary reasons. If Abigail couldn't care for her child, the last thing they wanted was for her to take her baby and run. The next place she left the infant might not be as safe. They had a responsibility, but Grace could see how difficult that separation had been for both mother and baby.

Abigail adjusted Taylor in her arms, looking down at her tenderly and sniffling back her tears.

"I was scared…"

Grace kept silent, waiting.

"I wasn't doing very well with Taylor. I… I was getting so frustrated and angry, and Taylor would cry and cry. And I couldn't go out and do anything, and my boyfriend left me and said I was a bad mother." Tears welled in her eyes. "And I just thought maybe I could get a fresh start and just be a teenager again!"

"So you decided to bring her to an Amish home?" Grace asked. "Was that because of your Amish family?"

A lot had come to light the last few hours, including that she had Amish family in the community of Redemption. Abigail knew their names, and the name of their community, but she'd never been in their lives.

"My mother was raised Amish," Abigail explained. "And there was this huge scandal. She and her husband didn't get along very well. She ran away and divorced him, and that got her permanently kicked out of the community. Anyway, she had me after that, and I didn't know my Amish family. We didn't visit them or anything. At least not that I remembered. There are some pictures of me on an old lady's lap—my grandmother." Abigail swallowed.

"So I thought that my baby would be safe at an Amish home, because you see Amish people in the market, and you hear about them. And their life seems so calm and peaceful. Unless they marry the wrong person, I guess."

Grace smiled faintly at that. What had this young woman gone through?

"You told us yesterday that you don't know any of them," Grace said.

"No." Abigail shook her head. "I don't know them. My mom was shunned, and she brought me back to see my grandmother once, but she said she couldn't do that again. Mom said that no mother in her right mind would—" tears welled in Abigail's eyes "—send her child to go where she herself wasn't welcome. She said that we were a package deal. We came together."

Grace nodded. "It's understandable."

"Yeah, it is." Abigail sighed, and she looked down at her daughter in her arms. "My mother wouldn't have understood what I did. She would have been so disappointed in me."

"Your mother died," Grace said softly. "And you were left very much alone. I think she could forgive you."

Abigail swallowed hard, then straightened her spine. "Does that mean I can go now?"

If only it were so easy.

"Where would you go?" Grace asked.

"I have friends. I'll figure it out."

"Are these the same friends who helped you to leave Taylor at the farm?" Grace asked.

Abigail was silent for a moment.

"They cared," the girl said, her chin trembling.

"Abigail, you left your baby in a basket outside someone's house in the middle of very cold weather. And then you drove away," Grace said. "We have to face that. Deal with it. You were very overwhelmed, and you didn't think you could be a good mother to your child."

"I'm feeling better now," Abigail said, pulling her baby closer. "It was a mistake. I missed her too much."

"I know, and I do appreciate that you changed your mind. I'm glad you did! It's a step in the right direction. But we can't just let you take your baby and go," Grace said. "We don't want to separate you from your baby, either. Please don't be afraid of that. We need to help you. We need to get you some support so that you don't get overwhelmed again. We have resources available."

Abigail was silent.

"I know that your mother passed away last

year," Grace went on. "Who have you been staying with?"

"Aunt Ruby—she's not really my aunt. She's one of my mom's old friends. But she's got her own kids to worry about, and I didn't exactly make everyone proud getting pregnant when I did." Abigail swallowed.

"You're listed as a runaway," Grace said. "So you weren't with Ruby most recently."

Abigail sighed. "No. I was staying with friends."

"Why did you leave Ruby's home?"

"Because we always argued," Abigail said. "She kept telling me I had to do this, or do that, or get a job, or think about the future, or...whatever. And I wasn't her daughter! I was just this pile of trouble because she was my legal guardian. That was it."

"And you don't want to live with Ruby now," Grace clarified.

"I'd rather not, but if there's no other way, I'd go back," Abigail said.

"Your grandmother—your Amish grandmother—has been located, and she's on her way to see you," Grace replied. "You knew her name—Cecily Peachy... And you said you saw a picture of her, right?"

Abigail dropped her gaze. "But I don't remember her."

"Do you want to meet her?" Grace asked.

"Do I have a choice?"

"Of course. She's not expecting anything from you. She's hoping to just introduce herself. But she might be able to help."

Abigail was silent.

"Have you ever thought about meeting your mother's family in Redemption?" Grace asked.

"I wanted to," Abigail said at last. "But my mother wouldn't let me."

"And after she died?" Grace pressed.

"I don't know. What do you say? Hi, I'm the kid you knew about but had no contact with, the daughter of the woman you shunned. And now my mom is dead. Just thought I'd drop in." Her tone dripped sarcasm.

"This is your chance to meet your grandmother," Grace said, ignoring the bait.

Grace's job was not an easy one, but the outcome for this case was more optimistic than most. They'd found the mother of the abandoned baby, and she wanted her child back. She didn't have addiction issues, she'd passed the psychological assessment. Her biggest problem was that she was very young and had little support.

Grace's desk phone rang, and she answered it.

"Grace Schweitzer," she said.

"Grace, we have Cecily Peachy here to see you."

"Thank you," Grace said. "Why don't you show her into the interview room?"

She hung up the phone and met Abigail's gaze.

"Your grandmother just arrived. She'd very much like to meet you. But no one is going to force anything. This is up to you."

Abigail dropped her gaze, and Grace could see the battle going on within her.

"If I don't like her?" Abigail asked at last.

"Then at least you've met her, and we sit down together and find some solutions to get you the help you need with your daughter," Grace said.

"You promise?" And suddenly Abigail looked younger than her teen years.

"I promise," Grace said gently.

The next couple of hours consisted of introductions. Cecily had only seen her granddaughter once when she was a toddler, and there was a fair amount of awkwardness between them. Grace brought the two women into a private room where they could talk in a more relaxed atmosphere, and then she went back to her office. She left her office door open so that she could see the door to the interview room, and heaved a sigh.

This girl had been raised English, and yet she had an Amish lullaby in her heart. She didn't know her Amish family, and yet they were the only ones left to be a support to her. The strain between the two worlds was a painful one.

Grace glanced at her watch. She had other things to take care of today, and it was time to sit down with grandmother and granddaughter and see if there was a workable solution so that this baby girl could grow up in a safe home.

Grace headed across the hallway, and she was about to push the door open when she paused. They were still talking.

"What will they do with me?" Abigail asked.

"I think they'll suggest that you come live with me, and I could help you raise little Taylor," Cecily said.

"Oh…"

"And if that were okay with everyone," Cecily said, "would you like to come?"

"I'm a mess, Granny."

"Call me *Mammi*," she said gently. "That's what you call your Amish grandmother."

"Then, I'm a mess, *Mammi*," Abigail said, her voice shaking. "I won't make much of an Amish woman. I hardly manage to pull it together in my life here. If you're thinking you'll turn me into some Amish housewife, think again."

There was silence for a moment. Then Cecily's soft voice came through firm and strong.

"My dear, an Amish life has nothing to do with perfection," she said. "It has everything to do with community, and that's because we need each other. *Gott* takes some who are strong, some who are dedicated, some who are intelligent, some who have forgiving hearts, and he sews them all together in a sort of patchwork quilt with the ones who are weaker, who need more support, who are still learning. That's what a community is, and it is ordained by *Gott*. You don't have to be perfect, or even halfway good at being Amish, my dear. You just have to be willing to try. I'm not perfect. I never was able to sort out my relationship with your mother, and it's a lifelong regret. But maybe *Gott* has brought me you so that we can help each other."

The words echoed inside of Grace's heart. It was a beautiful description of the Amish life, but did it work in a practical sense? Grace couldn't help the little jump of hope inside of her.

"Help you with what?" Abigail asked.

"Oh, just be needed, I suppose."

There was a pause, and Grace was about to open the door when Abigail said, "And if I still don't want to be Amish?"

That was the question, wasn't it? Would Cecily, whose daughter had been shunned, accept a granddaughter who chose an English life? How far would her acceptance go?

"Then you'd have to be willing to live with me and work hard at raising your daughter to be a kind, loving, productive member of society," Cecily said. "And we'll let *Gott* sort out the rest."

"You really want me to come, don't you?" Abigail asked.

"My dear girl, you and Taylor are all I have left of my own daughter," Cecily said. "I want nothing more. And I hope you'll like me more than you think you will. I'm not sure what your mother told you about me... about us..."

"I think I should get to know you myself, don't you?"

Grace cleared her throat and pushed open the door. Cecily sat on the edge of a cushioned chair, her dress hanging low, revealing black boots. She was a short woman, rather square in shape, with a creased, wise face. Abigail didn't look anything like her grandmother, but there was a certain way of holding their heads that seemed similar between them.

Grace gave them each a bright smile.

"I hope you'll forgive me, but I overheard that perhaps you'll be willing to raise Taylor together?"

Cecily looked over at Abigail, her expression schooled into calm, but Grace could see the anxiety in the older woman's eyes.

"Yes," Abigail said. "Would you let me bring my baby with me? You won't stop us?"

Grace suppressed her own sigh of relief.

"We think that's a good solution," Grace said gently.

The paperwork needed to be completed and house calls set up for social services to visit and check up on the situation. There were doctors' appointments to arrange for the baby and mother, and all sorts of little details to sort out. Grace took it upon herself to discuss the necessity of regular doctor visits for all of the women—from infant all the way up to grandmother.

"I'll make sure that Abigail and Taylor see the doctor," Cecily assured her.

"And you, too," Grace said earnestly.

"Please, it's important. They need you to be healthy, too."

Cecily looked unconvinced. "I'm pretty strong."

"We all are," Grace said. "But this isn't about strength of character or morality. This is about your health and your longevity. It matters. Trust me—I've seen a lot in this job."

And in her personal life.

"Well, I suppose you would, wouldn't you?" Cecily agreed, and Grace saw something change in the older woman's eyes. Was it Grace's experience on the job that had swayed her?

But even while Grace worked, her heart was pounding with new hope.

If Amish life was about all sorts of people knit together into a community, if there was room for a single mother in desperate need of guidance and structure, was there room for her to go back? Would there be space for an Amish woman with a college education, career experience with the English and a deep belief in a woman's right to see a doctor regularly?

Because seeing this world-weary girl get a chance to live with her Amish *mammi* had filled her own heart with sympathy and… dare she say it…a righteous kind of envy.

Grace wanted to go home, too, but "home" had taken on a new meaning inside of her. Grace's heart was filled to overflowing with one man. He needed an Amish wife. Hope flickered inside her that she could be that wife in his arms. Was there any hope for a life with Ben?

Standing on the sidewalk outside the brick building, Ben double-checked the address on the business card Grace had given him. The taxi ride into Vaughnville had been a tense one. Coming out to see her was a step of faith, and he'd prayed the entire way that *Gott* would give him the right outcome. If Grace was indeed the woman for him, then let her accept him, because the thought of living without her now was too painful to even consider.

But if she wasn't the woman for him...let *Gott* be his comfort, because he would need it.

The snow on the sidewalk had been shoveled aside, and the warmer weather seemed to be melting the city. The cars sent up a mist of water as they passed, and Ben headed through the office building's glass doors.

Social services was on the third floor, so he took the elevator up, his palms sweaty. When the doors opened on a warmly lit office with a middle-aged woman at the front desk, he felt a wave of uncertainty. Imagining Grace's *Englisher* life was different than seeing it.

"May I help you?" the woman asked.

"*Yah*, I'm here to see Grace Schweitzer," he said. "My name is Ben Hochstetler."

"Ah. Yes, about the Amish case, I presume," she said with a nod. "Come this way."

The Amish case? Was this about Taylor's mother? He followed the woman down a hall, and then she tapped on a door and poked her head in.

"There is a Ben Hochstetler to see you, Grace?" the woman said.

"Oh!" Ben heard her exclamation through the door, and he attempted to hide his smile. "Yes, let him in…um… Ben?"

Ben stepped forward. The professional, poised woman suddenly looked flustered, and her face grew pink. She nodded quickly to the other woman and beckoned him inside.

Ben shut the door behind him and looked around the office. There was a desk, some file cabinets, a picture on the wall of a field of wildflowers. There were several leafy green potted plants around her office, and he was reminded of her descriptions of her plants on her balcony at home.

"I missed you," Grace said at last.

"*Yah*, me, too," he said. "And I had this all thought out before I left, and I memorized it on the ride into the city, and now that I'm here, I don't remember how to say any of it."

"Really?" A smile came to her lips. "Try."

"I—" He swallowed. "I came here to convince you to marry me."

That wasn't how he'd wanted to say it, but it summed it up rather nicely.

"What?" Grace searched his face. "Are you serious?"

"To be perfectly honest, I also had to convince you to come back and live with me. Because I can't live out here—I'm Amish, after all." Why was this coming out so badly? He shut his eyes for a moment, licking his lips. "Let me start over."

She nodded. "Please do."

And he gathered her into his arms and kissed her. This said it better. This was easier, somehow, than putting it all into words, because his love for her wasn't easy to articulate. She leaned into his arms, and when he was quite done, he broke off the kiss and looked down into her eyes hopefully.

"I love you," he breathed. There. That was better. "I love you, and these last days with you lit up my life in a way I've never experienced before. I saw the type of woman you are—kind, fun, resourceful. But most important, you pray...and that means more to me than anything, because I believe in prayer. So I love you, and I'm not going to try to stop loving you. I prayed for *Gott* to take away these feelings if you weren't for me, and... well, I only love you more. So maybe that's my answer! I want you to come back with me, marry me and be my Amish wife."

As crazy as that sounded standing here in her *Englisher* office.

"Is there any way you would let me take care of you?" he pleaded. "I'll provide. I'll make sure you see as many doctors as you want, whenever you want. I'd never hold you back! I want you with me until we're old and gray and wandering confused down the road together."

"You'd have to see a doctor regularly, too," she said.

"Me?" Somehow he hadn't thought of that. But her expression was serious.

"*Yah*, you!" she said. "If we're going to be old and gray together, you'll have to see doctors, too. Your health matters as much as mine."

"Then, *yah*," Ben said. "I'll go."

"Okay," she said.

His heartbeat sped up. "So, will you marry me, Grace Schweitzer?"

"You're proposing to a woman in a pantsuit," Grace whispered.

Ben swallowed, then nodded. "*Yah*... I am."

"I might be terrifyingly liberal," she added, her expression sober.

"This is where those prayers come in," Ben said. "I'll pray just as earnestly as you do, and we'll let *Gott* lead us. Together. In everything. Besides, name one thing that would scandalize me with your liberal ways. Besides the pantsuit."

He tugged gently at the top of her lapel, a smile tickling the corners of his lips.

"I'm going to try to convince the entire community to see the doctor for yearly visits," she said. "And that's the truth. I won't stop. I won't let up."

Ben thought for a moment, then nodded. "Okay. We'll both see the doctor every year, and so will the *kinner* that hopefully *Gott* will bless us with."

"You're making this very easy," she said. "Are you sure about this, Ben?"

That was the right question, because suddenly his nerves calmed. Was he sure? Crazy as this would seem to everyone he knew and loved, yes, Ben was absolutely sure.

"I love you," he said quietly.

"I love you, too."

"Good. And you keep praying like I saw you that night. Grace, that is all I need. If you'll come back and be my liberal, Amish, praying wife, I'll be happier than you could ever know."

He watched her face, the surprise, then the warmth in her eyes, the blush in her cheeks. For a moment all was still. It was like the whole world was holding its breath, and then she nodded.

"*Yah*, Ben," she said. "I'll marry you."

He gathered her back into his arms and kissed her again—this time out of sheer joy.

"Good!" he said when he pulled back. "And the sooner the better. Now that I've found you, I don't want to wait any longer than absolutely necessary."

There was a tap on the door. "Excuse me, Grace?"

Grace smoothed her suit and took a step back. "Yes, come in."

The door opened, and the same woman from before appeared, but she had an Amish woman Ben knew at her side. Cecily Peachy. Ben blinked in surprise, and Cecily looked equally shocked.

"Cecily?" he said.

Cecily had a young woman in blue jeans at her side, and the young woman had little Taylor in her arms. Cecily and the young woman came inside, and the receptionist retreated.

"Ben. Hello. Meet my granddaughter, Abigail," Cecily said.

"So Taylor's mother..." His mind whirled through the possibilities. "Is your granddaughter?"

"My daughter, Leah, left her husband eighteen years ago—do you remember that?"

"*Yah*, of course," he replied. It had been a scandal back then, and Paul Ebersole had lived with his brother's family ever since.

"This is her daughter, Abigail," Cecily said. "She'll be staying with me for the next few years, and we'll be raising Taylor together."

"That's wonderful," he said. "I'm really glad to hear it."

"And I think..." Cecily said, looking over at Abigail hesitantly. "I think it's time that Abigail met her *daet*."

Ben stared at the older woman. "Paul Ebersole doesn't know about her?"

"There have been secrets for too long," Cecily said. "It's time for it all to come out. And she has a living parent. She deserves to meet him."

Secrets, indeed. *Gott* had truly been working in that storm. Ben blew out a breath, and when he glanced over at Grace, he found her looking just as surprised as he felt. And then they exchanged a smile.

"Cecily, do you think I could meet you and Abigail in the waiting room?" Grace asked. "I just need another couple of minutes."

As Cecily and Abigail left, Grace closed the office door and put a hand against her chest. They both started to laugh as their eyes met. None of that mattered right now for the two of them. He'd marry this woman, bring her home and love her so thoroughly that she'd never question her choice to be his.

Somehow, through all this trouble, *Gott* had sorted out a solution that was so blessedly generous to Ben that he could hardly believe it.

"Maybe we could go get something to eat," he said quietly. "Once you're done here."

"Yah," Grace said softly. "I'd like that."

There were wedding plans to make, decisions for their future…maybe a visit to her family. Whatever was in store, she'd be at his side, and his heart soared.

Gott was good. There was no other way to explain it.

Epilogue

Grace and Ben arrived at the Schweitzer farm in Creekside, Pennsylvania, in the middle of a bright, cold morning. Grace's teenaged brothers, Nate and Jacob, were just coming back inside from chores when the taxi pulled up, and they stopped to watch in curiosity. It took them a moment to register that it was their older sister who got out of the vehicle first while Ben paid the driver, and the boys whooped out their joy and ran toward her for a hug.

That brought her two younger sisters, Gloria and Liza, out of the house, too, and Grace hugged all of them.

"How long are you visiting?" Jacob asked.

"And you'd better not argue with *Mamm* this time," Liza added with a nervous laugh.

"I'm not arguing with *Mamm*," Grace reassured them. "And I think we'll stay for a couple of days... I've got news."

Grace heard the car door slam behind her, and all four of her siblings froze, their attention locked over her shoulder. Then their surprised gazes whipped back toward Grace.

"Who's he?" Nate demanded.

"Meet Ben," Grace said. "Ben, these are my brothers and sisters."

There were introductions, and Grace understood why they were confused. She was dressed in her regular work wear, and Ben was very obviously Amish. She had a lot of explaining to do today.

Grace looked up to see her mother standing on the step to the house, her arms crossed over her middle. Her hair was grayer now than it had been when Grace visited last year, and she looked a little plumper, too.

"Hi, *Mamm*," Grace said.

"Come on inside," her mother said. "It's cold out."

The explanations took time. Ben chatted with her siblings in the kitchen, and Grace and her mother went to the sitting room to talk. There was much to discuss, much to understand. And the news of the engagement brought a flush to her mother's cheeks and a tremble to her chin.

"I prayed, Grace," she said. "Oh, how I prayed! And I don't know if I was praying for the right things or the wrong things, but I needed our daughter back."

"I know, *Mamm*," Grace said. "Thank you for that."

Those prayers that had seemed so narrow and focused had been charged with the love and longing of a mother. Grace didn't resent their specificity anymore, either. She was glad to come back—to have it all again.

"So you're coming back to Amish?" her mother asked hopefully.

"Yah, *Mamm*, I'm coming back," she said. "I had to find my own way. I'm sorry this was hard on you, but I still believe *Gott* took me on my own journey."

Her mother dropped her gaze. "Maybe He did, my dear. But as your mother, watching my child leave everything I so lovingly gave her—" She swallowed hard. "Your journey wasn't easy on me. One day soon you'll have a baby girl of your own, and I think you'll understand a little better."

"I probably will," Grace said softly. "I love you, *Mamm*."

Her mother squeezed her hand. "If you're coming back Amish, why aren't you dressed properly?"

Grace looked down at her work wear—a charcoal pantsuit, a silk blouse. She knew how it looked—uncommitted, English.

"Because I wanted to spend a couple of days here with you," Grace said softly, tears welling in her eyes. "I didn't want to wear dresses sewn by others. I don't know if that's silly or not, but… I hoped you'd sew some dresses with me."

"Oh…" Her mother's eyes widened. She leaned forward, wrapped her arms around Grace's neck, and rocked her back and forth a couple of times. "*Yah*, I'd love that. We'll make you four dresses—I've got plenty of material, and I'll send you with some of my own stockings, and we'll get you your *kapps*, and your aprons… Oh, Grace. We're going to fill your hope chest just as fast as our fingers will work!"

"And, *Mamm*," she added softly. "Just to make me happy, could we talk about you getting a doctor's checkup?"

Her mother sighed, her earlier excitement seeping away. "It's so expensive. I took your siblings a couple of years ago, and maybe it's time to take them again. But it costs so much, and some things I'd rather not know."

"Please…it's important, *Mamm*. We need you around for a long time. I need my mother.

I know it's scary. But it's…it's a way to keep you around. Okay?"

Her mother licked her lips. "I'll discuss it with your *daet*."

It was a start. There would be more talks, but maybe they'd get further now.

The side door banged, and Grace's father's boots could be heard in the mudroom. He was back from the fields, and the explanations, hugs, tears and relief started all over again. When all the stories had been told for the umpteenth time, he reached out and shook Ben's hand.

"Welcome to the family, Ben," her father said, and then he lowered his voice, tears sparkling in his eyes. "And thank you for bringing my daughter home."

"My pleasure," Ben said, and his voice caught. "Really. From my heart. It's my earnest pleasure."

Grace smiled at her fiancé, and they exchanged a look filled with promise and hope. She'd found her way home again. But home meant something a little bit different now. Home was now about her husband-to-be, about their new life together and their dedication to each other.

Home had grown, spread and embraced a whole new family along with her own. And

Gott had answered all of their prayers with one very timely snowstorm. May He lean close and continue to listen to their heartfelt prayers, because the adventure was only beginning.

* * * * *

If you enjoyed this story, be sure to pick up these previous books in Patricia Johns's Redemption's Amish Legacies series:

The Nanny's Amish Family
A Precious Christmas Gift
Wife on His Doorstep

Available now from Love Inspired.

Dear Reader,

Mothers and daughters have seen the world through different eyes since time began. Mothers love their daughters fiercely, and daughters take their own paths. The stronger the mother, generally speaking, the stronger the daughter, too! In this book, I wanted to look at a relationship between a mother and a daughter—both of whom are strong-minded, are certain that they're right, and humble themselves to pray. I truly believe that prayer makes all the difference, even when things seem most impossible.

If you enjoy this book and want to see more of my backlist, come by my website at PatriciaJohnsRomance.com. Come find me on Facebook, too. I have constant giveaways going on with other fantastic authors. I'd love to see you!

Patricia Johns

Get 4 FREE REWARDS!

We'll send you 2 FREE Books plus 2 FREE Mystery Gifts.

Harlequin Heartwarming Larger-Print books will connect you to uplifting stories where the bonds of friendship, family and community unite.

FREE
Value Over
$20

YES! Please send me 2 FREE Harlequin Heartwarming Larger-Print novels and my 2 FREE mystery gifts (gifts worth about $10 retail). After receiving them, if I don't wish to receive any more books, I can return the shipping statement marked "cancel." If I don't cancel, I will receive 4 brand-new larger-print novels every month and be billed just $5.74 per book in the U.S. or $6.24 per book in Canada. That's a savings of at least 21% off the cover price. It's quite a bargain! Shipping and handling is just 50¢ per book in the U.S. and $1.25 per book in Canada.* I understand that accepting the 2 free books and gifts places me under no obligation to buy anything. I can always return a shipment and cancel at any time. The free books and gifts are mine to keep no matter what I decide.

161/361 HDN GNPZ

Name (please print)

Address   Apt. #

City   State/Province   Zip/Postal Code

Email: Please check this box ☐ if you would like to receive newsletters and promotional emails from Harlequin Enterprises ULC and its affiliates. You can unsubscribe anytime.

Mail to the Harlequin Reader Service:
IN U.S.A.: P.O. Box 1341, Buffalo, NY 14240-8531
IN CANADA: P.O. Box 603, Fort Erie, Ontario L2A 5X3

Want to try 2 free books from another series? Call 1-800-873-8635 or visit www.ReaderService.com.

*Terms and prices subject to change without notice. Prices do not include sales taxes, which will be charged (if applicable) based on your state or country of residence. Canadian residents will be charged applicable taxes. Offer not valid in Quebec. This offer is limited to one order per household. Books received may not be as shown. Not valid for current subscribers to Harlequin Heartwarming Larger-Print books. All orders subject to approval. Credit or debit balances in a customer's account(s) may be offset by any other outstanding balance owed by or to the customer. Please allow 4 to 6 weeks for delivery. Offer available while quantities last.

Your Privacy—Your information is being collected by Harlequin Enterprises ULC, operating as Harlequin Reader Service. For a complete summary of the information we collect, how we use this information and to whom it is disclosed, please visit our privacy notice located at corporate.harlequin.com/privacy-notice. From time to time we may also exchange your personal information with reputable third parties. If you wish to opt out of this sharing of your personal information, please visit readerservice.com/consumerschoice or call 1-800-873-8635. **Notice to California Residents**—Under California law, you have specific rights to control and access your data. For more information on these rights and how to exercise them, visit corporate.harlequin.com/california-privacy.

HW21R2

HARLEQUIN SELECTS COLLECTION